WHEN I WAS THE GREATEST

OTHER BOOKS BY JASON REYNOLDS
The Boy in the Black Suit

WHEN I WAS THE GREATEST

JASON **REYNOLDS**

ATHENEUM BOOKS
FOR YOUNG READERS
NEW YORK   LONDON   TORONTO   SYDNEY   NEW DELHI

Special thanks to Elena Giovinazzo and Caitlyn Dlouhy.
And, of course, my family.

ATHENEUM BOOKS FOR YOUNG READERS
An imprint of Simon & Schuster Children's Publishing Division
1230 Avenue of the Americas, New York, New York 10020
This book is a work of fiction. Any references to historical events, real people, or real places
are used fictitiously. Other names, characters, places, and events are products of the author's
imagination, and any resemblance to actual events or places or persons, living or dead, is
entirely coincidental.
Text copyright © 2014 by Jason Reynolds
Cover photograph copyright © 2014 by Michael Frost
Sculpture of knitted gun copyright © 2014 by Magda Sayeg
All rights reserved, including the right of reproduction in whole or in part in any form.
ATHENEUM BOOKS FOR YOUNG READERS is a registered trademark of Simon & Schuster, Inc.
Atheneum logo is a trademark of Simon & Schuster, Inc.
For information about special discounts for bulk purchases, please contact
Simon & Schuster Special Sales at 1-866-506-1949 or business@simonandschuster.com.
The Simon & Schuster Speakers Bureau can bring authors to your live event. For more
information or to book an event, contact the Simon & Schuster Speakers Bureau at
1-866-248-3049 or visit our website at www.simonspeakers.com.
Also available in an Atheneum Books for Young Readers hardcover edition.
The text for this book is set in Arno.
Manufactured in the United States of America
First Atheneum Books for Young Readers paperback edition August 2015
10 9 8 7 6 5 4
The Library of Congress has cataloged the hardcover edition as follows:
Reynolds, Jason.
When I was the greatest / Jason Reynolds. — First edition.
pages   cm
Summary: Ali lives in Bed-Stuy, a Brooklyn neighborhood known for guns and drugs, but he
and his sister, Jazz, and their neighbors, Needles and Noodles, stay out of trouble until they go
to the wrong party, where one gets badly hurt and another leaves with a target on his back.
ISBN 978-1-4424-5947-2 (hc)
ISBN 978-1-4424-5948-9 (pbk)
ISBN 978-1-4424-5949-6 (eBook)
[1. Conduct of life—Fiction. 2. Family life—New York (State)—Brooklyn—Fiction.
3. Brothers and sisters—Fiction. 4. Neighborhood—Fiction. 5. Violence—Fiction.
6. African Americans—Fiction. 7. Brooklyn (New York, N.Y.)—Fiction.] I. Title.
PZ7.R33593Jer 2014
[Fic]—dc23 2012045734

"Be good to your family, y'all,
no matter where your families are
'cause everybody needs family, y'all . . ."

—Yasiin Bey (Mos Def),
"Sunshine"

"Okay, I got one. Would you rather live every day for the rest of your life with stinky breath, or lick the sidewalk for five minutes?" Noodles asked. He turned and looked at me with a huge grin on his face because he knew this was a tough one.

"It depends. Does gum or mints work?"

"Nope. Just shit breath, forever!" He busted out laughing.

I thought for a second. "Well, if I licked the ground, I mean, that might be the grossest thing I could ever do, but when the five minutes was up, I could just clean my mouth out." In my head I was going back and forth between the two options. "But if I got bad breath, forever, then I might not ever be able to kiss the ladies. So, I guess I gotta go with licking the ground, man."

Just saying it made me queasy.

"Freakin' disgusting," Needles said, frowning, looking out at the sidewalk. "But I would probably do the same thing."

A sick black SUV came flying down the block. The stereo was blasting, but the music was all drowned out by the loud rattle of the bass, bumping, shaking the entire back of the truck.

"Aight, aight, I got another one," Noodles said as the truck passed. He shook his soda can to see if anything was left in it. "Would you rather trade your little sister for a million bucks, or for a big brother, if that big brother was Jay-Z?"

"Easy. Neither," I said, plain.

"Come on, man, you gotta pick one."

"Nope. I wouldn't trade her."

Another car came cruising down the street. This time, a busted-up gray hooptie with music blasting just as loud as the fresh SUV's.

"So you tellin' me, you wouldn't trade Jazz for a million bucks?"

"Nope."

"You wouldn't wanna be Jay-Z's lil brother?" Noodles looked at me with a side eye like I was lying.

"Of course, but I wouldn't trade Jazz for it!" I said, now looking at him crazy. "She's my sister, man, and I don't know how you and your brother roll, but for me, family is family, no matter what."

Family is family. You can't pick them, and you sure as hell can't give them back. I've heard it a zillion times because it's my mom's favorite thing to say whenever she's pissed off at me or my little sister, Jazz. It usually comes after she yells at us about something we were supposed to do but didn't. And with my mom, yelling ain't just yelling. She gives it everything she's got, and I swear it feels like her words come down heavy and hard, beating on us just as bad as a leather strap. She's never spanked us, but she always threatens to, and trust me, that's just as bad. It happens the same every time. The shout, then the whole thing about family being family, and how you can't pick them or give them back. Every now and then I wonder if she would give us back, if she could. Maybe trade Jazz and me in for a little dog, or an everlasting gift card for Macy's, or something. I doubt she'd do it, but I think about that sometimes.

Me and Jazz always joke about how we didn't get to choose either. Sometimes we say if we had a choice, we would've chose Oprah for a mom, but the truth is, we probably still would've gone with good ol' Doris Brooks. I mean, she's a pretty tough lady and she don't always get it right, but there's no doubt that she loves us. And we know we're lucky, even when we're getting barked at. Plus, it's not always about us. I mean, sometimes it is, but other times it's about other things, like our mom just being stressed out from work. She's a social worker, and all that really means is that she takes care of mentally sick people. She makes sure they get things they need, kind of like being a step-step-stepmother to them. At least that's the way she breaks it down to us. I could see how that could be stressful, so Jazz and I do the best we can to not add to it.

What's crazy is that we don't ever really see our mother that much anyway, mainly because she also has another gig at a department store in the city. So she works with the mentally ill from nine to five, and then sells clothes to folks who she swears are just plain crazy, from six to nine thirty, and all day on Saturday. Sunday she takes off. She says it's God's day, even though she spends most of it sleeping, not praying. But I'm sure God can understand that she's had a long week. I sure do.

Mom says the only reason she has to work so hard in the first place is because our rent keeps going up. We live in Bed-Stuy, and she's always complaining about the reason they keep raising the rent so much around this part of Brooklyn, is because white people are moving in. I don't really get that. I mean, if I'm in a restaurant, and I order some food, and a white person walks in, all of a sudden I have to pay more for my meal? Makes no sense, but that's what she says. I don't really see the big deal, but that might be because no white people live on my block yet. And I can't see none moving around here no time soon either. Shoot, black people don't even like to move on this block. People say it's bad, and sometimes it is, but I like to focus on the positives. We got bodegas on both ends, which is cool, and a whole bunch of what my mom calls "interesting" folks who live in the middle. To me, that just equals a good time, most of the time.

A lot of the stuff that gives my neighborhood a bad name, I don't really mess with. The guns and drugs and all that, not really my thing. When you one of Doris's kids, you learn early in life that school is all you need to worry about. And when it's summertime, all you need to be concerned with then is making sure your butt got some kind of job, and staying out of trouble so that you can go back to school in September. Of course, Jazz isn't old enough to work yet, but even she makes a few bucks every now and then, doing her little homegirls' hair. The point is, Doris don't play with her kids fooling around in all that street mess. Lucky for her, I don't really have the heart to be gangster anyway. I ain't no punk or nothing, but growing up here, I've seen too many dudes go down early over stupid crap like street cred, trying to prove who's the hardest. I'm not trying to die no time soon, and I damn sure ain't trying to go to jail. I've heard stories, and it definitely don't sound like the place for me. So I always just keep cool and lay low on my block, where at least I know all the characters and how to deal with all their "interesting" nonsense.

Like my next-door neighbors, Needles and Noodles. They're brothers, and when you talk about having a bunch of drama, these dudes might be the masters. They're both my friends, but Noodles, the younger brother, is my ace. He's only younger than Needles by a year, so it's more like they're twins, but the kind that look different. Not identical, the other kind. And really, when I think about it, Noodles actually is more like the big brother in their house, but only because Needles's situation, which I'll get to, makes it hard for him to do certain things sometimes.

I met them almost five years ago, when I was eleven, after the Brysons left the neighborhood. The Brysons were an old couple who lived next door, who everyone loved. Mr. Bryson had lived in that house since he was a kid, and when he met

Mrs. Bryson on a Greyhound bus coming from the March on Washington, a story he used to tell me all the time, they got married and she moved in that house with him. They lived there until they were old, and out of the blue one day they were gone. Not dead. Just gone. They moved to Florida. When they got there, they sent me a postcard from their new home. On the front was a picture of Martin Luther King Jr., and on the back it said, in Mrs. Bryson's handwriting:

> *Dear Allen,*
> *We had a dream too . . . that one day we wouldn't*
> *have to take the "A" train ever again. Our dream*
> *has come true.*
> *With love,*
> *The Brysons*

I never heard from the Brysons again, and after they left, their brownstone got grimy. I don't know who took it over, but whoever it was, they didn't care too much about nothing when it came to who they let live there. All kinds of wild stuff started happening up in there, from crackheads to hookers. I guess the easiest way to put it is, it became a slum building—a death trap—which was crazy because it was such a nice place when the Brysons had it. Then one day Needles and Noodles showed up. Well, really just Noodles. It was a Sunday morning, and I was running to the bodega to get some bread, and when I came out the house, Noodles was sitting on my stoop. I had never seen him before, and like normal in New

York, I ignored him and went on about my business. But when I got back from the store, he was still sitting there.

We made eye contact and sort of did the whole head-nod thing. Then he spoke.

"Yo," he said. His voice was kind of raspy. I noticed he was holding a crumpled ripped-out page of a comic book, and a little pocket-size notebook that he was scribbling in.

"Yo," I said. "You new?"

The guy looked exhausted, even though it was the middle of the day. The sun was baking, and sweat was pouring down his forehead.

I glanced down at the comic. Couldn't recognize which one it was, which didn't surprise me. They were never really my thing.

"Yeah," he said, tough. He quickly folded the colorful paper up and slid it between the pages of the tiny notebook. Then he smushed it all down into his pocket.

"What floor?" I asked. I was a little confused because I didn't think anybody had moved out.

"Second." He tugged at the already stretched-out collar of his T-shirt.

I laughed but was still confused. I guess I just figured he was joking.

"Come on, man, I live on the second floor, so I know you don't live there."

"Yeah, I live on the second too," he said with a straight face. "Over there." He nodded his head to the house next door. The death trap.

I was stunned, but I knew better than to make it weird.

"So what you doing over here?" I asked, putting the grocery bag down on the steps.

"Sitting," he muttered, staring at the next step down. "Would you sit on that stoop if you was me?"

Hell no, I thought. Noodles explained that he couldn't stay all cooped up in that place, so he came outside to get some fresh air. But then he realized he also didn't want nobody to think he lived there, so his plan was to sit on my stoop until it got dark, and then slip back into his own building. I wasn't sure what to say. I didn't want to start nothing because he seemed tough, and I didn't know him yet. He looked mad, and I couldn't help but think that wherever he came from was much better than this place. Had to be.

"I'm Ali," I said to him, holding my hand out for dap.

He looked at it as if he was trying to figure out if he wanted to give me five or not. Then he reached out and grabbed it, our palms making that popping sound.

"Word. Roland."

"It's cool if you chill out here," I said, like I owned the building or something. As if I could stop him from sitting on the concrete stairs.

The two of us sat on the stoop for a while. I wanted to ask him what comic he was reading, but judging by how fast he folded it up, that didn't seem like a good idea. I don't think we talked about anything in particular. I just remember acting like a tour guide, pointing out who was who and what was what on the block. I figured it was the least I could do, since he was new around here. The hard part was trying not to point to his house and say, "And that's where all the junkies stay."

The sun had gone almost all the way down, and the streetlights were flickering, when my mother poked her head out the window to call me up for dinner.

"Who's that, Ali?" she asked, sort of harsh.

"This is Roland. Just moved in . . . next door," I said, looking up at her, trying to drop a hint without being too obvious. Roland turned around and leaned his head back so he could see her too.

"Hi, son," my mother said, the tone of her voice softening. I could tell that she was as surprised as I was to know that he was living in the slum building.

"Hello," he said sadly.

Doris looked at him for a moment, sizing him up. Then she shot her eyes back toward me.

"Ali, can you bring my bread inside!"—I totally forgot!—"And come on and eat before this food gets cold," she said in her usual gruff tone, but then turned toward Noodles, and said all nice and kind, "and you're welcome to come eat too, sweetheart."

As we ate, my mother asked him where he was from, but he avoided answering. Then Jazz, who at the time was only six, picked up where Doris left off and started interrogating him, asking him all kinds of crazy stuff.

"Your mom don't cook?" she asked. My mother shot her

a look, and before Noodles even had a chance to answer, Jazz changed the question.

"I mean, I mean," she stumbled while looking at Doris out the corner of her eye, "you like SpongeBob?"

"Yeah." The first time he smiled all day.

"Dora?" Jazz questioned.

"Yep."

"*The Young and the Restless*?"

"Of course," Noodles said, unfazed. Then he broke out laughing. He was obviously joking, but Jazz decided right then and there that she liked him.

After dinner he helped me wash dishes and thanked my mother for letting him come up and eat. Before he left, he pulled out his tiny notebook and scribbled a sketch of SpongeBob, that kinda looked like him, and kinda not, but it was still pretty good just from memory. Jazz had already left the table and was washing up for bed, so he told me to give it to her. And once it got dark enough outside, and quiet enough on the block, he made a dash into his apartment.

Though we weren't really friends yet, he was the first person I ever had come over to hang out. I don't really have any homeboys in the neighborhood, just because a lot of teenagers around here are messed up these days. Either they're selling or using, and the ones that aren't are pretending to, or have overprotective mothers like Doris who don't want their kids hanging with nobody around here either. I have a few dudes I chill with at school, but I never really get to see them too much during the summer, just because most of them live in Harlem and I almost never go there. And they definitely don't come to Brooklyn. So I had no choice but to keep the friends to a minimum—until Noodles.

The next morning I looked out the window, and sure enough, Noodles was sitting out there on my stoop. I remember watching him pop his head up from a different torn comic-book page, and his notepad, to watch the kids play in the hydrant. I got dressed fast and ran out to see what was up.

I guess he didn't hear me open the door, because he flinched, big-time, when I said, "Yo, man."

"Yo, you scared me. Don't be creeping up on folks like that. Get you messed up, man." He didn't laugh, but I did. But once I realized he didn't, I stopped. Then he laughed.

"What's that?" I looked at the comic and the small piece of line paper covered in blue ink.

"Oh. Incredible Hulk," he murmured while folding it up in the mini pad.

I could tell he was a little embarrassed about the comic thing—maybe he thought I would think he was some kind of geek or something. I didn't really see what the big deal was. If you into comics, you into comics. And even though I wasn't, I knew who Incredible Hulk was. Who didn't?

"Aw, man, Bruce Banner a bad dude," I said.

He opened the notepad and handed it to me.

It was one of the scenes where Bruce was upset and was turning green and becoming the Hulk. Noodles had literally redrawn the whole thing perfectly, every muscle, every hair. The only difference was he drew a Yankees hat on the Hulk, but it looked like it belonged there. The kid could really draw! Noodles said it was one of his favorites, but when I tried to give it back to him, he ripped the page out and told me I could have them both, the comic and the sketch.

He was on my stoop every single day after that, sunup to sundown. Noodles probably wouldn't have been the friend my mom would've picked for me, but she felt sorry for him, plus Jazz liked him, so Mom made sure there was always extra food for him every night.

Luckily, a couple weeks later the dude who owned that building finally straightened up the outside of the apartment. A new door and some new windows. Everybody in the hood was talking about how the inside was probably still a piss pot, but at least it didn't look as bad from the outside. At least Noodles could sit on his own stoop without feeling some kind of shame. Plus, I could sit with him, which was cool because I was getting tired of always sitting on my stoop all the time.

I bet you're wondering how he started getting called Noodles. Well, if you ask him, he'll say he was given that name by the hood, just because he always tries to be hard. But the truth is, it came from Jazz, who's pretty much the master of nicknames. As a matter of fact, she's the person who started calling me Ali. My real name is Allen, but that's not where Ali comes from. Jazz gave me Ali after one of my boxing lessons from old man Malloy, who I'll tell you about later. I remember leaving Malloy's house, running down the block, busting into our apartment all gassed up, excited to show Jazz what I learned. I was bouncing around the living room, bobbing and weaving, punching the air all silly. I think Malloy had just taught me the left hook, and I hadn't really got it down yet, so my arms were flying all over the place. Jazz laughed her head off, and made some joke about how I could be the next Muhammad Ali, as long as I keep fighting air and not real people. I won't lie, that stung a little bit, especially since she knew I was kinda scared to have any real matches. But whatever. From then on, that's what she called me, Ali, and then everybody else started to, too.

Noodles's nickname story is better than mine, though. Jazz liked him a lot, especially after *The Young and the Restless* joke, and the SpongeBob drawing, which she had taped to her wall. Every time they saw each other after that, which was pretty much every day, they would crack jokes and tease. One day she found the perfect ammunition. She saw Noodles out the window kissing some butt-ugly girl on the stoop—Jazz's words, not mine. She told me that the girl was twice Noodles's size and looked like she was trying to eat his face, and she couldn't tell if the girl was our age, or if she was an old lady, dressed like a girl our age. She said Noodles looked so scared, and that his lips were poking out and puckered so tight that it looked like he was slurping spaghetti. The next time Jazz saw him, she rode him hard about it, squeezing her lips up like a fish. At first Noodles tried to deny it. Then he said it was one of his mother's friends, and that it was more like a family-type kiss. Whatever it was, I wasn't about to ask no questions. I could tell he was pissed, and I was starting to figure out that he didn't take embarrassment too well.

I was worried that he would stop being cool with me. I mean, I still didn't know him that well for Jazz to be clowning him so bad. But I guess he had a soft spot for her, and if not her, a soft spot for dinner at my house. Either way, Jazz promised to never let it go, calling him "noodle slurper," and stuff like that, and after a while he ended up just getting over it. And that's how he got the name Noodles. Before that, he was just Roland James. That name is nowhere near as cool as Noodles, and even though he never gives my little sister credit, we all know he's thankful for it now, even if it is a funny story.

Okay, so as for Needles, he's only technically been called Needles for about a year, and his nickname story is nowhere near as funny as Noodles's and mine, but it is way more interesting. But in order for it to make any sense, I have to start at the beginning.

I didn't even meet Needles until about three months after I met Noodles, which I thought was weird. I mean, I knew Noodles had a brother, but I never saw him. I always wondered if he was forced to stay in the house, if he wanted to stay in the house, or if he was just someplace else, like with his father or something. All Noodles ever said about him was that he was kind of wild, which is pretty much what everybody always says about their brothers and sisters, so that wasn't a big deal.

When I finally met him, he was with Noodles. They were walking down the block, coming from the corner store,

Noodles ripping paper off cheap dime candy and tossing it on the sidewalk. I first gave Noodles some dap because I already knew him, and as soon as I reached for Needles's hand to introduce myself, he basically started cussing me out. Scared me half to death, I swear. I couldn't tell if this was some sort of joke, or if he just didn't like me, but I couldn't understand how he could not like me when we didn't even know each other yet. But after he finished dogging me, he said, "Wassup, man" in a superquiet voice like he was scared but cool. He also apologized for coming at me that way. That really confused me. And then, to top it all off, Noodles slapped him in the back of the head. I didn't think that was cool, but I didn't know them well enough to be standing up for nobody.

So yeah, I thought Needles was a little bit weird, but when I told my mom about it, she made it clear, and I do mean clear, that there was nothing funny about Needles's condition. She said the proper term for it is Tourette syndrome. So I guess it's a syndrome and not a condition. She said that what happens is he blurts out all kinds of words whenever his brain tells him to. Not regular words like "run" or "yo" but crazy stuff like "buttface" and "fat ass." I figured that's what Noodles meant when he told me that Needles was "wild."

My mother told me she had a girl on her caseload who suffered from it, and that once people learn to manage it, they can usually live normal enough lives. But judging by the way Needles acted when he spoke, and how Noodles slapped him around, I could see it being tough to, especially since it had to be pretty embarrassing.

As the months turned to years, everybody pretty much got used to Needles and Noodles, especially me. I would say we were like the three musketeers, or the three amigos, but that's so played and has been said a million times. My mother said we were the three stooges, and Jazz said we were the three blind mice, but whatever. The point is, we were almost always together. Every holiday, they would come over for dinner. Every birthday, we'd dish out birthday punches (mine always hurt the most). And every regular day, we would just hang on the stoop. When school was in, I had to be upstairs by the time the streetlights came on, but summer, I could hang pretty late as long as I was out front. They never had a curfew, so they were always down to kick it. We would play "Would you rather," talk trash about girls, and I would talk about sports, but neither of them knew anything about athletes, so I spent a lot of time just schooling them. Noodles would read his comics and draw in his book, and Needles, who at the time was still known as Ricky, would kick freestyle raps about whatever he saw on the street. Like, if it was a bottle on the sidewalk, he would rap about it. Or if it was a girl walking by, he would rhyme about her. And believe it or not, he was pretty good, even with the occasional outbursts that, for me, had become so normal that it was like they weren't even happening. One rap I always remember is, "Chillin' on the stoop, flyer than a coop, stay off the sidewalk, 'cuz there's too much dog poop." And then, out of nowhere, he screamed, "Shithead!"

Even when we weren't together, we were. See—and this

is gonna sound weird—but our bathrooms shared a wall, and I don't know if it was because of water damage or what, but the wall was superthin. You could hear straight through it, and it wasn't like we were spying on each other using the bathroom—that wouldn't be cool—but sometimes we'd talk to each other through the wall whenever we were washing up. When it was Noodles, we wouldn't really be saying too much, just asking if the other person was there. I don't know why. It was just always cool knowing someone else was there, I guess. And I always knew when it was Needles, because I could hear him in there rapping and talking all kinds of crazy stuff, cussing and whatnot. Whenever he was rapping, I'd make a beat by knocking on the wall, until Doris or Jazz came banging on the bathroom door, telling me to cut it out. The point is, we were always, always, always together. That's just the way it was.

Most of our neighborhood accepted Needles for who he was. No judgment. I mean, it's New York. A man walking down the street dressed like Cinderella? That's nothing. A woman with a tattoo of a pistol on her face? Who cares. So what's the big deal about a syndrome? Whatever. It's in our blood to get over it, especially when you're one of our own, and by that I mean, when you live on our block.

Noodles was the only person always tripping about Needles. Despite the head swipes, Noodles was super-protective over his brother, and paranoid that people were laughing at him. He would always be shouting at somebody, or giving dirty looks to anyone he thought might be even thinking about cracking a joke about Needles. It was like he lived by some weird rule, that only he could treat Needles bad, no one else.

But nobody was ever really laughing at Needles. There was never a reason to. Needles did sweet things that were normal, just not always normal around here. He would help old ladies get their bags up the steps, ticking and accidentally cussing the whole way, calling them all kinds of names, but they didn't care because everybody had gotten used to it. They knew he couldn't help it, and that he was fine. Some of them would even give him a few dollars for his help.

But there were these times when Needles would sort of spaz out, but not like Noodles, who would just trip over any little thing. Needles's was more like mini meltdowns. It was like a weird part of the syndrome where every now and then his brain would tell him to have an outburst, but it wouldn't tell him to stop. So he would just go wild, cussing and screaming, over and over again, rapid-fire style. And even though folks around here was cool with Needles, the freak-outs were the only times people really looked at him like he was, well, crazy. I can't lie, the first time it happened, even I was shook up watching Noodles basically drag Needles into the house, giving a middle finger to all of us looking at his shouting brother like he was some kind of animal.

About a year ago Needles had one of these fits—a bad one. It was a Sunday, and my mother was by the window and heard a bunch of commotion coming from outside. She looked out and there Needles was, sitting on the stoop next door, going off like nobody's business! I mean, he was really going for it, calling out all kinds of "screwfaces" and "ass-mouths" and whatnot. By this point I'd seen him lose control tons of times, but it had never been as bad as it was that day. The worst part about it is there was a crowd of people gathered there, just listening and staring. Some were even laughing under their breath, and this time Noodles wasn't around to shut it down.

My mother was pissed. I mean, really mad. I ran behind her as she stormed downstairs, and let me tell you, when that door flung open, those people met the worst side of Doris Brooks. She ran toward the crowd like she was getting ready to start swinging on folks, and people started walking away pretty quickly. I laughed a little bit, only because I was used to my mother being pretty scary, especially when she feels like someone is being treated wrong. After all the people left, she walked over to Needles, who was still shouting random stuff. She gave him a hug. He told her thank-you in his soft voice, and explained that he was locked out of the house. He was crying.

My mother figured that she might know something that could help him. She's no doctor, but she is a mother and that means something. Plus, it's pretty much her job as a case worker to know stuff about different kinds of syndromes and stuff like that. She told Needles to stay right there, and told me to wait with him while she ran back upstairs. I wasn't so cool with that, only because he was really buggin', but I knew I'd better do it before Doris got busy on me. Besides, he was my friend, so I stayed, even though I did wonder where Noodles was and why he left Needles out there like that.

When she came back, she had one of those black plastic bags you get from the bodega. I thought to myself, I know she ain't bring this boy a leftover hero and some chips. And I was right. She didn't. She brought him something even more crazy—a ball of yarn and some knitting needles. What in the world? I tried to ask what she was planning to do with those, but she shushed me before I could get it out.

"You ever seen this, Ricky?" she asked, holding up the ball of yarn with the long silver needles jammed through it.

"Yes, ma'am," he said, embarrassed.

"Do you know what to do with it?" she asked. I thought to myself, of course he doesn't. I don't even know what to do with it.

"Uh, not really. I saw an old lady on the train doing something with yarn and those things, but I don't know what," he said, shy.

Then he blurted out. I couldn't really make out what he said. My mother didn't even flinch. She gave me a look. The look.

"Okay, well, let me show you. I think it'll help. Is that okay?" she asked. She wasn't speaking to him in any sort of "slow" way. Just talking pretty regular but being sure to ask a bunch of questions. It didn't seem like a good idea to try to force him to do anything in this particular situation.

He shook his head and worked to get out a soft "Yes."

So my mother took the yarn, which was purple, and the

two knitting needles, and started to show Needles how to knit. Knit! Like somebody's grandma! Now, I didn't even know my mother knew how to knit. She never knitted nothing for me and Jazz. I didn't even know where the yarn came from. Turns out, it was something that she had learned a long time ago from her mom, and she was planning to teach Jazz how to do it, sort of as a passing-down-of-traditions type of thing, but she never had time to, with all the jobs.

"Okay, first you have to hold the needles," she said, "like this." She held the two needles in her hands the way my little sister used to hold her fork and knife when she was really hungry as a toddler. Like a caveman. "Got it?" she asked Needles, who had gotten real quiet—just twitching a little.

He looked at her hands for a few seconds, then positioned his hands just like hers, except he wasn't holding any needles yet. He looked up at my mother to make sure he was doing it right.

"Like this?" he asked.

"Yep. Just like that, Ricky. Very good," my mom said, smiling. By now my butt was hurting, so I stood up. I knew I couldn't go home because my mother would have had a fit, so I just leaned on the shiny new door and kept watching.

"Now, this part is tricky, but you can handle it. It's called casting on." My mother took the ball of yarn and tied a knot on one end. She slipped it on one of the needles. Then she started looping yarn around the needle until the whole thing was covered. Seemed pretty easy to me.

Needles leaned in, closer, staring. It's funny how some

people's eyes talk more than their mouth does. Needles is one of those people. His eyes say all kinds of stuff.

"Did you see what I did?"

"Yeah, I saw it," he said.

"You sure?"

He smiled. "Yep." His voice was still soft, but now it had a little happy in it. He nodded.

"Okay. Now watch closely, Ricky. I'm gonna make a stitch." She took the needles and did something that I can't really describe because of where I was standing. All I know is, it made a stitch.

"And here's another one," she said, repeating what she had just done. Now there were two stitches. I acted like I didn't want to know nothing about knitting, but honestly, it looked kind of cool. Like, at first it was just yarn, but now it was turning into something else.

"See?" she said to Needles while making another stitch. And another one. And another one.

Needles's eyes were following along. He nodded and moved his hands as if he were the one holding the needles. I couldn't tell if he was getting it or not, but he kept saying he was. I wasn't—it looked pretty tricky. Not to mention, judging from the size of those stitches, it would take Needles the rest of his life just to make a sweater.

Needles shouted out again, "Shit breath!" while slowly moving his hand toward my mom. I perked up a little just to make sure he wasn't about to try no wild stuff, because even though I ain't no bad dude, I know enough about throwing a punch to put him in check. I mean, he was my boy, but I had never seen him this out of control before. But my mother stayed calm. He moved his hands until they were on top of hers. Then he slowly wrapped his fingers around the needles, and my mother released her hands. Next thing I knew, Needles was holding the needles.

My mother smiled. "Go ahead, Ricky."

He started to move his hands around, almost as if he was trying to recall the movements my mother had been making with her hands before he took the needles. Then, like it was nothing, my man Needles started knitting up a storm.

His eyes were so big, like he couldn't even believe what he was doing, but he was doing it. You know when you have to smile but you don't want nobody to see you smile, but it almost hurts to hold it in, so it comes out like a weird smirk? Needles did that weird smirk.

I just stood there with my mouth wide open. I couldn't believe he figured it out, just like that.

I looked at my mother.

"What?" she said. "Oh, let me guess, you want me to show you how to knit now too?"

"Who, me? Naw, I'm good. That's all Ricky. I ain't trying to be looking like nobody's granny out here," I shot back. She knew I was just playing tough, though.

"Uh-huh. Okay, Al. You bad," she teased. She stood up and brushed the cement dust off her butt. "Aight, I'm headed in."

"Me too," I said quickly. I knew that wasn't really cool of

me, but I was kind of nervous to just be sitting out there with Needles without Noodles being around. Not that day. "Later, Ricky," I said, walking over to the next stoop, which was mine.

When me and Doris got upstairs to our apartment, Jazz was sitting in the window drinking a glass of iced tea and working on her scrapbook, which was one of her favorite things to do. She started scrapbooking when my mother found all these old pictures of her and my father and me and Jazz from back in the day. My mom decided to get an old photo album to store them all in, and put Jazz in charge of doing it. But Jazz, being Jazz, decided to do her own thing and started cutting the pictures up, taking John, my father, from one, Doris from another, and maybe her and I from a different one. Then she'd cut out a page from a magazine, maybe of a beach, or somewhere overseas like Paris, and glue the cutouts of us to the picture. Like a bootleg, imaginary, family vacation photo. It was kinda cool. When Doris first saw what she had been doing with the photos, she was pissed that Jazz was cutting up the pictures. But then as she looked more, seeing us in random places we had never been, like Africa, she laughed and thought it was pretty cute. But soon the sight of seeing us all together like that, her with my dad, page after page, turned Doris's laughter into tears.

"Sorry," Jazz said, staring at what she thought was something nice.

"No, baby," my mom replied, smiling despite her wet face.

"It's fine. I love it." It was obviously a soft spot for Doris, and after that, she never really looked at Jazz's scrapbook again.

Jazz had been cutting and glueing, looking down on the whole thing, and was now watching Needles knit his heart out.

"What were you teaching Ricky how to knit for?" she asked as soon as we walked in. She put her glue stick down, turned the glass up to her face, and shook a piece of ice into her mouth.

My mother walked over to the sink and washed her hands while looking out the window at Needles, still going.

"Because it might help him. If he focuses on knitting, he might not have so many outbursts."

"Yeah, he might not say stuff like, Jazz is a cornball," I teased, looking over her shoulder at what she was working on. Us in Las Vegas.

"Ali," my mother said warningly. Jazz looked at me, crunched on the ice in her mouth, and smiled, because she knew she had won without even saying anything back. But I really wasn't trying to beat her.

"Jazz, it's like when you used to have a loose tooth, ready to come out. And I always had your brother come and pinch your arm. You'd be so concerned about Al pinching your arm that you would forget all about the fact that I was pulling a tooth out your mouth. And before you knew it, it was over."

"And I got a dollar," Jazz bragged. "From you, the fake tooth fairy."

I laughed and shook my head.

"The point is, Ricky will be so focused on what he's doing with his hands, that he won't worry about anything happening with his mouth. Understand?"

"Yep. I think I get it," Jazz said, turning to look out the window again. "Look at him down there, knitting. I can't even believe it." Then it hit her. "You know what I'm gonna start calling him? Needles. Yeah, Noodles and Needles"—she paused—"I like that."

★ 2 ★

Okay, so about Needles. I won't pretend he was a master-mind knitter or anything. I mean, he would just sit there on the stoop every day, in the middle of what had to have been the hottest summer ever, speaking in his soft way to all the neighbors walking by, freestyling, and knitting. But it's not like he was making something. He was just knitting to be knitting. Every time he would make a stitch or two, his arm would jerk and the stitches would come loose. See, the syndrome sort of moved from his mouth to his hands, as long as he was holding those needles. So my mother was right, he wouldn't blurt out crazy wild stuff as long as he was knitting, but his body would jerk instead. Every few minutes his arms would just shoot out in any direction. You never knew when it was coming, and you never knew in what direction they were going. But every time it happened, he would have to redo the whole knitting thing from the beginning. That would've made me crazy, but not Needles. He'd just start all over again like it was no big deal.

But something was bugging me—it was bad enough Needles was sitting outside in the middle of the summer, in the hood, knitting, but what made it worse is that he was using purple yarn. Like . . . purple. How could my mother be so smart, and not even question what that might look like? Anyway, me and Noodles took care of it. The first chance we got, we went and found him some black yarn to mess with. Well, we didn't exactly find it. We went and bought it, which by the way, was quite a situation.

The first thing we had to figure out was where to get yarn from. It's funny. When you don't know nothing about something, you really don't know where to even begin to find stuff that goes with the thing you don't know nothing about.

I threw out a few suggestions, like the hardware store, or the grocery store, but none of them were really making any sense. Then Noodles had a brainstorm.

"I know where we can get some," he said suddenly. We were walking up the block, headed toward Fulton Street. Fulton Street has all the shops, from wig joints to rib shacks. They even got a spot that sells TVs, Jamaican flags, leather jackets, and incense all in the same place. So we knew that if there was going to be a store that had yarn, it was going to be on Fulton Street.

"We can go check the pet store," Noodles said. He was pretty confident about this suggestion, but it made absolutely no sense to me.

"The pet store? What you talking about?" I said.

"Yeah, fool, the pet store. Ali—cats. They play with yarn."

He looked at me and bugged his eyes out. "Do they or do they not play with yarn?"

"They do."

"Aight, then. Let's do it."

The pet store was really only half a pet store. Not even that much. It was really a barbershop, and the dude who owned the shop, Brother, also sold animals and pet food and stuff like that. The only reason Noodles and I knew this is because Brother cut Noodles's and Needles's hair, and lined me up whenever I needed. Brother pretty much cut everybody's hair in our neighborhood. He was mean with the clippers. He could even make a young dude like myself, with no beard, look like I got a little something.

So we walked up to Fulton until we got to Brother's. The sign on the door said WELCOME TO BROTHER'S BARBERSHOP, WHERE EVERYONE IS FAMILY. Inside, the place smelled like a zoo. Dogs and cats and little gerbils in cages. And then there were the barbers. Farthest from the door was Trini, an old man from Trinidad who we all thought might be a barber, even though he never cuts anyone's hair. He also never says anything. I mean, nothing at all. He just cleans his clippers all day long. Next to him there was Cecil, who's pretty much the guy who cuts the old heads. He does that razor shave stuff with the cream and the towels. All the old guys come in and go to him only because they think Brother is going to make them look too young. And then closest to the door was Brother. Brother is a pretty regular-looking guy with a crazy thick beard that's always picked and combed perfectly. It kind of looks like he straps it on every morning. Brother always smells like oils and incense, and he's always kicking black facts to everybody. And even though he is always ranting about politics, he's still a cool dude, and everybody respects him because he has the cheapest cuts in town. Plus, he's known for busting a head or two if your lip gets too loose on him.

"Young brothers, young brothers, what's good?" Brother said as we came through the door. There was a few other people in the shop hanging out, waiting for cuts.

"Sup, Brother," Noodles said, giving him a pound with his fist.

"What's good, Brother," I followed up, playing cool as usual.

"Same ol' thing. Seeing red, being black, and making green, baby." We didn't know what that meant, but we never really knew what Brother was talking about when he said stuff like that. We just assumed it had something to do with being black.

"What y'all into today?" he said while brushing hair off the neck of the man in the chair, who was knocked out, asleep.

"Not too much, man, just trying to find some yarn," Noodles said.

Now, when he said it, I kind of froze up. I didn't think he was just going to blurt it out in front of everyone, plain as day, like it was a regular thing for two young Bed-Stuy dudes to be doing, let alone doing together. Everybody looked at us. Trini even took his eyes off his clippers and looked over at us. Awkward.

"Yarn?" Brother asked. "You mean like old-lady knitting

yarn? What y'all young brothers doing, joining a nursing home?" Everyone started laughing because that's pretty much what you do in the barbershop. You laugh at the barber who cracks jokes on the folks who come in. It's the rule. Once this guy came in and said he was selling his R&B album. Brother told him that he couldn't sell it in his shop unless he advertised it properly. Then he gave the poor guy a lecture on black business and how we need to do better, while Cecil gave him a history lesson on James Brown and Ray Charles. Next thing you know, that fool was doing a full-blown concert in the barbershop. Needless to say, everybody laughed. As a matter of fact, they laughed him out of there, but not before they bought a few of his albums, just to support.

"Yeah, man, some yarn. But it ain't for us," Noodles said.

"Of course not," Brother replied. We could tell he was being funny. "So who is it for, then? Your grandma?"

I could see Noodles start to get a little upset.

"No, it's for my brother," he said. He balled up his fist and looked around the room. "Now what? Laugh!"

Everyone was quiet.

See, even though Noodles seemed to always give his brother a hard time, he wasn't too cool about letting other people do the same thing. Like I said, he could slap Needles in the back of the head all day, but if Joe Blow from down the block did it, Noodles would flip his lid. And he was known for flipping out. I've seen him throw a whole pizza on the floor in the pizza place, just because they forgot to give his brother a soda.

But that's not why everyone was quiet in the barber-shop. I mean, Noodles had a big mouth, but he couldn't take on those old heads. They would've mopped him quick. The reason they all got quiet is just because they respected Needles. They knew he had a syndrome, but they also knew he was a good kid. He didn't bother no one or nothing like that. Plus they knew it wasn't cool to laugh at nobody with a syndrome, because you know, anyone's baby could be born with one, and if you laugh, you're pretty much begging God to give your next kid something like that. At least that's how I look at it, which is why I don't laugh.

"Easy, Noodles. No need to get upset." Brother tried to calm Noodles down. Trini looked back down at his clippers. "Let me run to the back and see if I got anything."

The back was where Brother kept all his pet supplies. It was basically a closet full of cat, dog, hamster, and fish food, leashes, flea powders, and a few toys like bones and rubber fire hydrants that make squeaky noises. Brother was quite the businessman.

"Sorry, young brothers"—Brother came from the back—"I got nothing."

"It's cool, man," I said, now speaking for Noodles, who was still cooling off. "Anybody know where we can get some?"

"Atlantic and Court," one older guy blurted out. "It's called Knit Wit." He paused and noticed all the other guys looking at him with a side eye. "Or something like that."

"And how exactly do you know this, Larry?" Brother was getting ready to go in on him.

The older guy, Larry, started shifting positions in his seat like his butt was heating up. He looked like he wanted to run out of the shop when he said, "My wife, man. She makes me go sit in with her at these knitting classes."

The shop broke out in laughter again.

"She makes you go? Yeah, right! You love it!"

"You volunteer to go, don't you?"

"You make her go sit in with you!"

"I want a Kwanzaa sweater with a pair of clippers on it. Got me?"

And on and on. Noodles and I left Larry to be eaten by the wolves and headed to Atlantic Ave. We figured we could just jump on whatever bus was coming and ride it down to Court Street. While walking toward the bus stop, Noodles had another bright idea.

"Aight, so how about when we get to the store, we just take some yarn, man. I mean, ain't no point in buying something so stupid," he said. I pretty much expected him to say this, but I knew it had nothing to do with yarn and was really all about him not having money to buy it. He would never just come out and say it.

"Yo, man, do you not know Doris? She would kill me!"

The bus was coming. Noodles didn't say nothing else about it, but I could tell it was still on his mind.

On the way to Court Street, Noodles just looked out the window and chewed on his fingernails. He spit the nails on the bus floor. A boy toward the back of the bus had music playing from his phone. The girl next to me was arguing with someone on hers. A baby was screaming in the front of the bus. Everyone was fanning themselves and wiping sweat, frustrated, trapped on the bus from hell.

Everyone except Noodles. He just sat there gazing out the window. He didn't roll his eyes or make some smart remark in typical Noodles fashion. He just stared and bit his nails. It was like he was out in space somewhere. When the bus finally got to Court Street, and I stood up to get off, Noodles didn't move. I had to call his name to snap him out of it.

"Man, I was gone. My bad," he said, his raspy voice even raspier, like he had just woke up. "We here?"

"Yeah, we here."

Noodles drifted off all the time. He never said what he was thinking about, and I never asked him because part of me was scared of what he'd say. He's the type of dude who could be daydreaming about anything, from doing something crazy like sticking up a place, or something cool, like making sure his brother's taken care of. Or, like in this case, both.

Court Street was like a whole other world than what we were used to. I had been there once or twice with my mom but never on my own. It's interesting how when you live in Brooklyn, you typically just stay in your own hood, unless you're going into Manhattan. But I know a lot of Brooklyn dudes my age who ain't never even been across the bridge. It's just one of those things.

There were shops everywhere, and I looked around for the knitting store while Noodles looked around for girls.

"Hey, Miss Yellow Shirt, I like them legs," he said. Then, when Miss Yellow Shirt looked at him sideways, he said, "You ain't even that pretty." Then he turned to me and said, "Yo, ain't no black chicks down here?"

To tell the truth, I was feeling kinda nervous about being in that neighborhood, and was more wanting to find the store than try to bag girls. After checking all four corners at Atlantic and Court Street, I finally had to break down and ask someone where the store was. I scanned the people waiting on the corner for the light to change when I saw an older woman who had that knitter look to her. And I was right.

"Excuse me, Miss, but do you know where a knitting store is around here?" I asked as politely as possible.

"Oh, Knit Wit, it's right over there. In the middle of the block," the older woman said. She pointed and smiled, and I just smiled back, a little embarrassed.

"Not for us," Noodles chimed in. "For my brother."

We walked down Court until we got to a door with a wooden sign with KNIT WIT painted on it. The words looked like yarn, which was kind of cool and kind of corny at the same time. It was obvious this was a place for old ladies.

The door opened, and we were greeted by a cat. That's not weird for stores in New York, but it just didn't seem like a good idea to have a cat hanging out in a yarn store. One bad day, and that cat could go bananas and shred the whole place. The fluffy kitty rubbed up against Noodles's leg, and Noodles halfway kicked it. He screwed up his face to purposely make himself look tough, like we had come to rob the place. But we didn't. At least I didn't. Just came to get some yarn. Black boys, looking for black yarn. That's it.

"Hello, boys," the lady at the register said. She didn't really have that knitter look the old lady who I spoke to outside had, but then again, neither does my mother. She had on a T-shirt and a pair of jeans with a hole in the knee. She also wore those hippie sandals that white people wear. My mother calls them Jesus sandals. Jazz calls them water walkers.

"Hello, how you doing?" I asked, trying to be mature and comfortable.

"I'm well, thank you. And yourself?"

I like when people say "well" instead of "good." Always sounds smarter. But I usually say "good." It just feels better coming out.

"Good, good," I said. I could feel things about to get awkward.

"So . . . what brings you in?"

"Our feet," Noodles said, just loud enough for her to hear. I nudged him.

"Oh, nothing much. Just looking for yarn," I said.

Hippie girl smiled.

"Of course you are." She held her arms out like she was saying, *Duh, there's yarn everywhere, dummy. It's a yarn store.*

"Yeah, but specifically, black yarn," I explained.

"You know what weight?"

"We'll just look around," Noodles snapped. It came off pretty rude.

I forced an uncomfortable grin as we turned away and

started walking toward the black yarn. The store was organized by color, so it was easy to see exactly where we needed to be.

"Why you being so mean, man? Lady was just doing her job," I asked Noodles while squeezing different yarns like they were cantaloupes in the grocery store. I didn't even know yarn had so many different feels. Weird.

"Man, who cares about her? Just trying to cuff one and bounce," Noodles said. "But we gotta get the right kind for Needles."

Again, I didn't say anything. I thought it was funny how even though he didn't want to be in the store looking for yarn because he didn't want nobody thinking he was soft, he still wanted to make sure he didn't just get any yarn, but the best yarn for his brother. And I could get with that. That's how I am with Jazz. She drives me nuts sometimes, but she's still my sister.

I watched as Noodles sized up the yarns to see which black was the best black for Needles. I saw him getting ready to make his move, so I stepped over to another part of the store, just in case hippie girl was watching.

Toward the back of the store there was a bunch of ladies gathered around a table. They were all knitting and talking and snacking on popcorn. Popcorn is my favorite. There was a piece of paper folded in half, the short way. It was propped up like a tent in the middle of the table. On it said THE CIRCLE. I didn't know there was such a thing. A knitting circle. I wondered if they were just a group of random women or if they were some sort of crew, like a sorority or something. Anyway, whatever they were, I figured they were just a bunch of ladies talking about lady stuff and knitting. But when I got closer, I overheard them talking about how someone named Susan got wasted the night before and that's why she wasn't there. I noticed an empty chair. Susan's. They laughed and went on about her and who she got with, and how much she drank, but they were talking about it like . . . us. Like dudes. It was cool.

"Excuse me, young man," a deep voice said from behind me.

I stepped out of the way of one of the biggest men I've ever seen. He sat down in Susan's spot. He had a beard and didn't look like no punk. Just a regular guy. He set his bag on the table. All the ladies were so happy to see him, laughing and blowing him kisses across the table. This guy clearly was the man.

I wanted to stick around to see if he was going to do what I thought he was going to do: pull out some yarn and start knitting like a girl, in which case I would've thought he had killer game, and gets all kinds of women because he can knit. Girls like stuff like that. At least I guess they do. But I never got to see what the big guy was going to do, because as soon as he started digging in his bag, I felt a tug on my shoulder.

"Yo, man, let's skate. I got it," Noodles said. He wasn't doing a great job at not being suspicious. He didn't even whisper. He pointed down. I looked, but I wish I hadn't. He had the ball of yarn stuffed in his pants. Not cool. Then, all nervous, he headed toward the door. He was walking so fast, he almost tripped over the cat. As soon as he pushed the door open, hippie girl caught on to what was going on.

"Excuse me," she said, and started coming from behind the counter. "Excuse me, young man?"

Noodles broke for it. I mean, he really took off. He couldn't run full speed because he had to hold his crotch to make sure the yarn didn't fall out. She went after him, but there was no way she was going to catch him. Not with them Jesus sandals on. I took my time and watched it all go down. Then I took five bucks out my pocket, laid it on the counter, and walked out.

★ 3 ★

You know how I knew Noodles wasn't really no tough dude? Two things. One, he was a comic book geek, and even though nobody else knew that, I did, and real bad dudes don't read comics, or draw them. And two, he ran his mouth too much. I don't mean just talking smack to people, even though he did do a lot of that, too. But what I'm talking about is, every time he did something bad, he would come back to the hood and tell the little kids about it, bragging like he accomplished something major. It's like he felt tougher whenever he started blabbing about it, gassing his own head up, turning the story into a much bigger deal than it really was. Bad dudes don't do that. They do dirt and keep quiet.

The worst part about Noodles always bumping his gums is that our neighborhood is like one big bubble of gossip. It's the telephone game we all played in elementary school, except not a game. Noodles tells a group of little kids playing in the hydrant about some stunt he pulled. One of those kids goes home and tells his mother about the crazy story Noodles told him. The mother tells her next-door neighbor, who tells another neighbor and another, the story changing, becoming worse and worse, until it finally, almost always, makes it to Doris Brooks.

"So, I heard a few days ago Noodles busted up in some shop, slapped a couple of old ladies around, took a whole bunch of stuff, and took off running. Heard the cops chased him and everything." My mother's voice was coming from her room. She was changing her clothes, getting ready to go to her second job. I was in the living room practicing my right jab–left hook combo in front of a full-length mirror I took from her room. "You know anything about that, son?" she said in that weird way that means I'm already in trouble.

My left hook went limp. It seemed like all of a sudden the sweat started to roll, and my stomach tightened up with nerves. She knew I was with him. I was always with him, ever since I met him. My best bet was to just tell the truth, but explain everything in a way that would keep me out of trouble.

"It wasn't all like that. No cops or slapping people or none of that extra stuff. Plus, I left the money on the counter," I said with fake confidence, still bouncing on my toes, with my guard up.

"But he tried to steal whatever it was?" she asked from down the hall.

"Yes," I replied reluctantly, feeling like I was snitching on my dude, but my mom had a way of getting the truth out of me. It mainly had to do with that cold look she always gave.

Surprisingly, she didn't get too upset about it. She came into the living room so she could see me. You know, look me in the eyes to see if I was being honest. She just stared at me for a second, sizing me up, probably thinking about whether she wanted to yell at me or not. Then she smirked and shook her head, bumping me out of the way so she could see herself in the mirror. She told me that she knew Noodles was my friend and that I was trying to look out for him. Then she said she would tell me not to hang with him because he's trouble, but that she knew it would do no good because she knew I would kick it with him anyway while she's at work. She told me she'd be kidding herself to think otherwise, and that she understood what it was like to be a loyal friend, and that she had bailed my father out time and time again the same way, until she just couldn't do it anymore. She said that when I got to the point when I couldn't do it anymore, when I couldn't take Noodles's foolishness anymore, I'd know it.

"And what exactly was that knucklehead stealing anyway?" she asked.

"Yarn. That part of the story is true," I explained, wiping sweat from my forehead. "We were at a yarn store. He was taking black yarn. For Needles."

She smiled, and I think she was trying to hold in a giggle. I could tell she couldn't believe it. Then she turned and walked back to her room. On the way she preached, "You know your father started off snatching small stuff too. And even though he said it was harmless, and that he was doing it for me, it didn't make a difference at the end of the day, because wrong is wrong. I know this story too well, Ali." She paused and then added with a sigh, "Too damn well."

It's like I could hear her shaking her head.

About my father. He's really not a bad guy. That's one thing my mother was sure that me and Jazz understood. He's actually a pretty good dude who just made some messed-up decisions. He wasn't into no drugs or nothing like that. And he also didn't beat on my mother neither. Doris don't play that. He was just a booster. He would go to different department stores and steal a bunch of clothes and then sell them on the street for cheap. Mom said he'd have dresses and shirts and pants, and whatever he couldn't sell, he would bring home to her. She says she still wears some of that stuff. He used the money that he made to pay bills while my mother was in school getting her social work degree. He also was saving a bunch of money so that he could take my mom on a trip. Like a honeymoon.

The issue was, he just wasn't very good at stealing and would get caught all the time. So my mother spent a lot of time down at the precinct, using up their honeymoon money to bail him out, which I think is another reason she has a hard time looking through Jazz's scrapbook. Seeing them on a beach, like on a honeymoon—pretty tough. Of course, the money ran out eventually, which meant rent couldn't get paid. So, my father started robbing corner stores. More money, faster. My mother said it was winter, and he would cover his face with a scarf, go into a random bodega far from where we lived, like in the

Bronx, and slip the cashier a note that basically said, "I don't want to hurt you. Just give me the money in the register."

And that was it. It actually worked a few times, and he'd come home and lie to my mother about where he got the money. And then one day she saw him on the news. He had tried to rob a store, and the guy behind the counter pulled out a gun and started shooting. My father shot back and hit the man in the chest. By the time my father got himself together to run, the cops were already outside.

The man in the bodega almost died, but he didn't, thank God. But my folks' relationship was pretty much over. My mother said she could not raise her kids with a man who was bound to either kill somebody or get himself killed. She says she couldn't allow herself to end up another sad story about a woman who stayed with a man who couldn't get himself together.

When all this was going on, I was superyoung, so I don't remember most of it. And Jazz was just a baby. He did three years in jail, and when he got out, my mother made it clear he couldn't stay with us anymore. She said she never stopped loving him and they still got together sometimes, but she knew she couldn't depend on him anymore. He just messed up too young. He never graduated from high school, and being in and out of jail made it hard for him to get back on course, and get a real gig. Doris says she doesn't think he ever really wanted to work a legit job. I know that's why she's so hard on me and Jazz about school and chores and staying out of trouble, and all that.

It's not like I never saw him, though. John came around all the time to check on us. He usually left a few bucks for Mom on the counter. She always split it between me and Jazz, but Jazz got the most during the summer, because once I got old enough, I worked a few mornings a week cleaning up for Mr. Malloy, so I got my own money. My dad tried not to come by when Doris was around because it was always so awkward, him knowing she loved him, but also knowing she couldn't deal with his crap. And I guess I could understand that since my mom and dad were pretty much married. That's a different kind of love. But I couldn't see myself getting tired of Noodles like that. Noodles was my main dude, and you never turn on your main dude. Really, when I think about it, he was my only dude. I knew Mom could somehow understand that.

A few days after the whole yarn-stealing incident, I went down the block to Malloy's house to clean up for him as usual, and to get some training in. The thing about Malloy is, he's one of those old-school Brooklyn dudes. One of those "Great-great-grandfather was born here, and bought a brownstone in exchange for a pair of steel-toe boots, and a pot of grits, and kept it in the family for a hundred years, and now Malloy lives in it to keep the tradition going" types of people, just like Mr. Bryson was, and actually, just like my mom is. It wouldn't surprise me if he was born in an alley, or behind a bodega. That Brooklyn. Lots of kids these days got Brooklyn tattooed on them, or talk mess to outta-towners about how Brooklyn they are, but they ain't nowhere near as Brooklyn as Malloy. Ain't nobody as Brooklyn as Malloy.

Malloy himself told me that he had never really even been out of Brooklyn except for the time he spent in the service. Army. Vietnam.

He was drafted. He said back in those days wasn't no black kids just signing up to fight. He said, "We wasn't that dumb, or that stupid." I always laughed when he said that. Malloy said, back then, he felt like the government was substituting all the poor black kids for the rich white kids when it came to serving in the war and that getting that letter in the mail, the one that said he had been drafted, felt like he was called from the far end of the home-team bench, asked to go in the game, and sucker punch the other team's star player. Take the rap. Be the bad guy. That's how Malloy always put it. He never went into too much detail about the actual war, though. I got the feeling he just didn't like talking about it too much. Once I asked him if he ever killed somebody, and all he said was, "Ain't grits groceries?" I took that as a yes.

One thing he loved talking about, though, was how Muhammad Ali didn't have to fight in the war. He always, always, always said how he respected Ali for standing up to the government, even though they put him in jail. I wonder what was worse, jail or war. Well, I guess if you're Muhammad Ali, one of the biggest stars and the best fighter ever, jail ain't so bad. I mean, it ain't like people were going to mess with the champ. Shoot, the biggest and ugliest dude in there was probably begging for Ali's autograph.

But for a regular Brooklyn Joe like Malloy, I'm not so sure. When I asked him what he learned from the army, he

said he learned discipline, brotherhood, and most impor-
tantly, how to box. Said he was the baddest boxer in his camp,
and couldn't nobody see him with the hands. Too fast. Too
focused. Floating and stinging, just like Muhammad Ali,
except he ain't sting like no bee, more like a Mack truck, he
bragged. Malloy always said the army was okay, but it was
the war that messed him up. Like I said, he never talked too
much about it, but one thing he never seemed to mind was
running down the story of what it was like waking up in the
medic tent with no legs.

"It's strange, still. It'll always be a little strange," he said,
his eyes looking away at something invisible. "You spend
your whole life running, paying attention to nothing but all
the dumb stuff, and then one day, while you running, something runs into you and leaves you with nothing." I really
didn't understand totally what that meant, but it somehow
made sense in some kind of way. The liquor on his breath
was always there, just like the tears caked and crusty in the
corners of his eyes. And he hated—HATED—for anyone to
try to ignore his legs.

His nubs didn't look like legs at all. They looked more
like giant fingers attached to his waist. When I first started
coming to his house, I would try not to look at them because
my mother taught me real early in life that it was rude to stare.
She said she'd slap my eyes off if she caught me. Picture that,
her slapping my eyes off! So when I first met him, I would
look all around the room, at his face, over his head, at the
floor, everywhere but his legs, until finally one day he said,

"Listen, the most important rule when you dealing with me is, the obvious should never be ignored." I didn't know how to take that statement, but I knew, early, that it was an important one. He followed up with, "Now look at them. It's okay. That way the pathetic legless elephant can disappear, and we can get the hell on with it."

His role in my life, according to Doris, was to be some sort of positive male figure. Go figure. But not just me, a lot of the kids in the neighborhood, mostly the ones without fathers in the house, would randomly pop up at Malloy's and talk to him about girls, and, well, mostly girls, and he would be there to listen and give some drunken but still pretty solid advice. My mother had known him since she was a little girl growing up in the same house I'm growing up in now. She said her father, my grandfather, Kirby, and Malloy were pretty much best friends, which is why she trusted him to look after me. She started sending me over there when I was around six; I guess she figured anything to keep me on the good path while John was locked up. Jazz was little and Doris probably just needed a break. Or some help. So one day she walked me down there. When Malloy opened the door, he looked at my mother's face and could probably see how tired she was. She always says it was like Malloy was reading her. There was no conversation about why she brought me there, or what she needed. Nothing like that. Malloy didn't even invite her in. All he did when he opened the door and saw us was squeeze my mother's hand and say, "Okay."

I've only been in one room in Malloy's house. The gym.

Which is really the living room. On the walls there are posters of boxers. Muhammad Ali, Joe Louis (who I found out later Malloy named his grandson after), Sugar Ray Robinson, Jack Johnson. It's just a big open space for sparring, and over on the side he's got a few dumbbells, a weight bench, a speed bag, and two punching bags, one hanging from the ceiling and one on a stand. The one on the stand is for him. No one can touch it. He keeps a permanent bottle of gin on a small, shaky wooden table in the corner, and a carton of Newport cigarettes next to it, along with a few military medals.

His face is like leather, and he usually keeps sunglasses on, even inside. He always wears an army T-shirt and old blue jeans, the thick, medium blue kind from back in the day. He knots them at the legs and cuts the extra fabric, which makes his legs look like denim sausages. It's strange to describe a person who doesn't wear shoes because he doesn't have feet. But he doesn't have feet.

The first time I went to Malloy's, as soon as I got inside, he asked for my hand. I gave it to him, and he shook it tighter than anyone had ever shaken it, and then he balled it up into a fist.

"Where's your father?" he said sort of rudely.

I couldn't believe that was the first thing out of his mouth. What a jerk, I remember thinking.

"I don't know."

"You know him?"

"Yeah."

"When's the last time you seen him?"

"I don't know." My mother told me to never tell people my dad was in jail. She didn't want people to judge us.

"Are you mad about that?" Malloy squeezed my fist tighter. "Are you mad at him, son?"

I didn't know what was going on. I started feeling scared. I was only six. Why was he grilling me with all these questions? Why was he squeezing my fist? I thought my mother just needed a break. A babysitter that was a man, so that I could have a strong man around since my father was locked up. Is this what strong men do?

"I don't know," I answered, stuttering.

"You don't know?" he said, confused. "Well, let me ask you this, let's pretend this punching bag is your father. What do you want to do to him?" He slowly released my fist. My nails were digging so deep into my palm that I thought I had broken the skin.

"Show me," he said again, this time nudging my shoulder.

I turned toward the punching bag, opened my fist, and wrapped my arms around it.

Malloy sat there in his chair staring at six-year-old me, hugging a punching bag like it was a person. He nodded his head like I had passed some sort of test.

"Okay. I got it," he said.

I stepped back.

"So you're not mad?"

"No, sir."

"Then I wanna teach you something." He took my hands in his and continued, "And I'm only gonna teach you because

I know you won't abuse it, like some of the other kids around here. You love first, and that's always a good thing. You're not fighting the war that so many of the other kids are fighting. You're rebelling against it, like Muhammad Ali. You know who that is?"

I shook my head yes.

"You're like him. Got a heart for people." He looked at me for a second with a funny smirk on his face. I'm not sure I really knew all of what was going on.

"Okay," I said. I had no idea where this was going, but I was hoping that eventually it would lead to a TV and a snack.

This time he balled both of my hands up into fists.

"I wanna teach you how to box, kid."

Now here I am, almost ten years later, still at it. Except I'm actually throwing punches now.

"Come on, Ali! Hit him!" Malloy barked as I threw my right jab at this kid, Jamaal Crowder. Jamaal was just another neighborhood guy that Malloy had taken under his wing. He didn't talk too much, and if I was his size, I probably wouldn't say too much either. I mean, who needs words when you're a teenage giant.

"Hit him!" Malloy commanded again, our shoes squeaking on the wood floor.

I threw another jab, one I knew was a stinger. It would've had any normal person doubled over, but Jamaal didn't even flinch nor did he wait for me to follow with another shot. He unloaded a flurry of body blows, backing me into a corner. I tried to defend myself by doing what Malloy had taught me. Block and counter. None of it was working.

"Punch! Don't slap him, son," Malloy said, annoyed.

The thing is, I knew what to do. I knew how to take cover and wait for the perfect time to throw the uppercut. I mean, Malloy had been training me for a long time, and it's not like I had never sparred before. I guess the stupid yarn situation was still bugging me—distracting me. I was just glad Doris didn't flip out about it.

"Okay, okay, that's it," Malloy murmured, saving me while trying to light a cigarette. "We're through. Good job." Jamaal backed off and held his gloves out for me to tap them with mine. A sign of sportsmanship and, thank goodness, a sign we were done. Don't know much more of the big guy I could've taken.

"How your hands?" Malloy wheeled over to me.

"Sore," I replied, pulling off the gloves and unwrapping layer after layer of the white tape Malloy always wrapped around my fists. He said it would toughen up my hands, but it didn't seem to be working.

Jamaal quickly tossed his equipment in a duffel bag and zipped it shut. He didn't say nothing. He just looked at me and Malloy, nodded, and headed for the door. He never hung around and helped clean up or talked trash with us. He just showed up, beat up on whoever was there, and rolled out.

Malloy shook his head, sort of confused, but instead of making some slick comment about how strange Jamaal was, he focused back on my hands.

"Let me see," he said, the cigarette dangling from the side of his mouth. I held them out. "This one here is swollen." He pointed at the middle knuckle on my right hand. "I don't know how many times I have to tell you—"

"I know, I know, keep my fists tight. Squeeze water out of a rock," I finished his sentence. I had heard it a million times.

"Your punch has gotten pretty solid over the years, but what you gonna do when you finally get in the ring, not for a spar but for a real match? Break your hands all up?"

Malloy took a pull on his cigarette and shook his head. Then he tapped the ash on the floor.

"Come on, man," I said, sucking my teeth. "I keep telling you I don't wanna fight nobody." I bent my fingers back to loosen them up.

"Hey, hey, don't get mad. I'm just saying." Malloy backed off, and rolled back over to the corner. "I ain't never met a boxer that's scared to box, that's all."

"It's not that I'm scared, I just ain't ready yet," I muttered, embarrassed. And totally lying. I was scared to death.

Malloy held up an empty bottle to see if there was anything left in it. Not much. Maybe a swallow. He shook his head like he was more disappointed in the bottle than he was in me.

"I know, Ali," he said, taking one more puff on his cigarette, then mashing it out. He blew a smoke stream up to the ceiling that seemed to go on forever, and then he looked over at me. "Aight, we're done for the day."

"But I didn't clean up yet," I said, confused. Usually it's training for an hour, then cleanup for an hour.

"Ah, it's Sunday. Don't worry about it," he said, twisting the cap off the bottle. "Just come by and do it tomorrow. I got things to do today." Yeah, like buy another bottle. Malloy took the last swallow and hissed. "Now go home and pray to God for some balls," he chuckled. I knew he meant it as a joke, but I didn't think it was funny at all. Low blow.

★ 4 ★

On my way back from Malloy's, I saw Needles and Noodles sitting outside on the stoop. The church up the block was just letting out. All the old ladies with the big hats and mustaches came stepping out like the sidewalk was a runway. The boys our age were all dressed in oversize suits, dingy shirts, and sneakers. The girls, in loose skirts and clunky shoes. There were a few old men in pastel suits, limping, I think, on purpose. They used white rags to wipe sweat from their foreheads and then stuffed them deep into their back pockets. There weren't many of them coming out of church, but the ones who were looked like they stepped straight out of an old movie. That's for sure.

Needles sat on the stoop, where he always sat. Two steps from the top. And he was doing what he was always doing, knitting, if that's what you want to call it. He held his needles awkwardly and wove in and out, looping the yarn slowly around each needle. Occasionally he would jerk, almost as if he were throwing a punch, and the loops would come loose. Same old thing. The black yarn seemed to be working out for him, though. He didn't look nowhere near as soft as he did with the purple. I knew my mom would agree once she saw it.

Noodles was standing, leaning against the railing. He was waiting for Tasha, like he always did every Sunday. Tasha was his girlfriend just because he said so. I don't know if they ever actually discussed this, or if she even knew she was Noodles's girl. But she was, let him tell it.

"Yo," I said, stepping up on the first step. "What's good?"

"The whole hood, understood?" Needles rhymed randomly. I snickered and shook my head while giving him dap.

"Wassup, man," Noodles said, looking down the block toward the church. But before I could say anything, he whipped toward me, covering his nose. "What the—damn, Ali, you stink! Where you coming from?"

"Man, I was down at Malloy's," I said, pulling my shirt up over my nose to get a whiff. It wasn't that bad. Noodles shook his head in disgust and went back to looking down the block.

"What you lookin' at anyway?" I asked, taking the attention off my funk. "Oh, let me guess, Tasha."

I put a whine in my voice when I said Tasha's name. Needles laughed.

Noodles stood on his tippy-toes and stretched his neck as if it would help him see clearer.

"Yeah, man," he said with an attitude. "She down there talking to some wack dude."

"How you know he wack? You don't even know that guy," Needles said.

"Plus, that's pretty much what people do after church. Stand around and talk to each other," I said, half-slick and half trying to make him feel better.

"Yeah, but not like she talking to him," Noodles insisted.

Needles sucked his teeth and went back to his yarn.

At first I wasn't going to look, just because I thought it was all so silly. But I couldn't resist. There Tasha was, standing in front of a man who I was ninety-nine percent sure was the preacher. The only reason I wasn't a hundred percent sure is because he didn't have on no gold or diamonds. Had he had on gold or diamonds, I would have been certain. He did have on the white collar, though.

"Man, you buggin'," I said to Noodles. "That dude's the preacher!"

I snickered to myself.

"Yeah, whatever. He just better not try nothing with my girl or I'm gonna have to Hulk up on him."

Now I had to choke back my laughter. I looked over at Needles, who was sitting behind Noodles. He smirked and rolled his eyes. Even he thought Noodles was acting silly.

After Tasha finished talking to the preacher, she started coming our way. I won't lie. Tasha was hot. On fire. She was grown-woman fine. Dark skin, long legs, big eyes, good teeth (she used to have braces), a mean walk, and a battery pack in her back full of attitude. But because of the rest of her, the attitude was easy to overlook most of the time. Plus, whenever she was dealing with Noodles, the smart mouth came in handy. She would fire right back and put him in his place like it was nothing. Tasha was like a flame, pretty to look at, but if you got too close, she'd burn you up.

"Hey, boys," she said, looking directly at Needles and me. "Oh, hey, Noodles," she grunted, and rolled her eyes around the world. It was clear she didn't count him as one of the "boys."

I said wassup.

Needles started, "Hey, Ta—"

"Tasha," Noodles cut him off, his voice already on ten. "Who was that you was talking to?"

"Oh, Lord," she said under her breath. "What you talking about?"

"That lame clown I saw you talking to down there. Who he? Y'all got a thing?"

Tasha smiled and put one hand on her hip.

"Do we got a thing? Oh, we got a thing, all right." I knew she was just teasing him, but Noodles bit like a pitbull on raw meat.

"Oh yeah? I knew you was cheating on me! Tell him next Sunday, church will be extended a few hours for his funeral," Noodles barked.

"Cheat on you?" Tasha bugged out her eyes like she couldn't believe what she was hearing. "Cheat on you? I can't cheat on someone I ain't with! Fool, you crazy!"

She twisted her mouth and squinted her eyes, making one funny, mean face. "Plus, that was my pastor, dummy. I ain't got nothing going on with him but trying to figure out how to get to heaven, which is what you need to be worried about too. You so busy chasing me. Better chase Jesus. Probably got a better shot!" Ouch. I was impressed. She really laid it on him with that one. It's not like he could say he didn't need Jesus or that he didn't want to go to heaven. Noodles is a bad dude, but he ain't that bad.

Noodles piped down. He knew he had been beaten again.

"What y'all doing out here anyway?" Tasha asked.

"Not much," I said, massaging my sore knuckles. Noodles was still in his feelings and tried to pretend that he didn't hear her.

Tasha shifted her weight to her other hip. "Wassup, Needles? Your knitting is getting good." Needles smiled so wide, you could see all of his teeth.

"Thanks, Tasha. I been sticking with it. I'm a make you something one day, watch," Needles said in his own smooth way.

"I know that's right, boy," Tasha flirted.

Noodles looked back at his brother and shot him a dirty look.

"What you into today, Tash?" I asked.

"Man, I gotta help Mo with his thing."

I glanced at Noodles. "What, Mo having another party?"

"You know it," Tasha said. She rolled her eyes again. I guess she wasn't too thrilled about helping out.

Mo, or MoMo as most of us called him, was her twenty-year-old brother. He was, pretty much, the coolest kid in our neighborhood. His claim to fame: secret parties. We had never been to one, but we, and probably every other kid in Bed-Stuy, had heard all about them. He had them in the basement of their parents' brownstone, and in order to come, you had to get a special invite, and know the secret code, which changed every time, to get in. This kid Matt I used to spar with at Malloy's went to one and told me all about it. Matt was older than me. I think he was eighteen, but he was built like a streetlamp, just like me. He used to give me the blues in the ring, so bad, but I still liked him. He was a good dude. You just never know if a person's lying or not, no matter how nice they are, but Matt said he went to one of MoMo's parties and claimed there were dancers there, and I don't mean ballerinas. I mean, dancers. Like, stripper dancers. And he said MoMo had arranged for a DJ to be there with the full setup. He said the DJ was playing behind the bar.

That's right, there's a bar at these parties too. With a bartender. I ain't too into the drinking thing, mainly because, well, I'd hate to come home trashed and Doris is there waiting for me with her mean face on. So I try to stay away from the liquor. But I thought it was cool that MoMo had it at the parties. Matt also told me that MoMo always had red lights, and that the girls that come to these parties ain't all uptight and stank acting. He even said he almost got some in the back room. That's right, MoMo has a back room down there too, just in case somebody gets lucky. Now, I didn't know if all this was true, but if it was, this was big-time, major-player type stuff.

The funny thing is, MoMo is nothing like the rest of his

family. His parents, Mr. and Mrs. Williams, were pretty much good when it came to money. Mr. Williams worked somewhere in the city. I'm not sure where, but I know he wore a suit and carried a briefcase every single day. I didn't even know people still carried briefcases, but I figured since he still was, there must've been some pretty important papers in it. Mrs. Williams is a biology professor at City College. The only reason I know that is because Tasha always talks about how she has to go to college, and how she's probably going to end up at City just because that's where her mom works and she can go for free.

Tasha's a straight-A student, and even though she always gave Noodles a whole bunch of lip, she was a cool girl. It's just that Noodles was always acting wild, so she had to put him in his place. That's all. But I knew she liked him. Sometimes you can just tell. It's the whole good-girl-likes-bad-boy thing, which I don't really get. Tasha's parents owned a whole brownstone that she says has been in her family for like seventy-five years. Kind of like the Brysons. She's the only person I know around here who still has one, other than Malloy, and it's cool that she doesn't try to make the rest of us feel bad about renting floors.

MoMo, whose real name is Maurice, on the other hand, didn't go to college. He didn't even finish high school. He doesn't have a job or nothing like that. But you would never know any of that if you saw him. He always walks like the sidewalk was put there just for his feet. His shoulders are always back, and he has this bop that I know he must've practiced for years to perfect. And to top it all off, the dude's got clothes straight out of a music video. Not just any kind of clothes. Clothes that looked like they'd cost a year's worth of morning chores at Malloy's.

Some people on our block assumed MoMo sold drugs. I didn't know if that was true or not, but it wouldn't have surprised me. Others said Mo's come-up was throwing those crazy parties that hood celebs and wannabes paid bank to get into. You know that place Studio 54 from back in the seventies? I heard that's what these parties were like, and the man behind the magic was MoMo. You would think that, with the hood talking as much as it does, it would get back to Mr. and Mrs. Williams. But it never seemed to because he usually only had them in the summer, which for him was prime time because his mother was on summer break, so her and Mr. Williams went on weeklong getaways, leaving the kids home. Party time.

"Word? Man, I'd love to go to one of Mo's parties. Everybody's always whispering about what goes on there," I said to Tasha. Noodles still had an attitude going, but I knew as soon as MoMo's party was mentioned, his ears turned on.

"Yeah, I know. Funny thing is, most of them suckers ain't even really been in," Tasha said.

"How you know?" Noodles asked suddenly. The dead had arisen.

"How I know?" Tasha's nostrils flared up. "Who you think works the door? Me, that's who. I see all the freaks, the hustlers, the crazies, all them. They all gotta come past me."

Tasha worked the door? Whoa—a crazy thought came to me. I stared at her, not quite wanting to say what I wanted to say, and she called me on it.

"What is it, Ali?"

I didn't say nothing. Just started looking at everything except her. The cars. The telephone wires. The fire hydrants. The kids running.

"Ali, what?" she said, louder.

Nothing.

"Oh no. Don't tell me." Tasha could sense what I was thinking. "Don't tell me you want to go. Please don't tell me that," she said, her voice kind of begging.

"No, *we* wanna go," Noodles chimed in perfectly, for once. He pointed to me, and then pointed back to himself, and grinned what I guess was his most charming grin.

Tasha looked at Noodles, then shot her eyes over at me.

"Y'all too young. You know that. I don't even get to really go in. I just gotta sit in the front part and take money and all that."

"Yeah, but you can just wave us in. We'll tell you all about it." Noodles, now coming out of his slump, leaned forward excitedly. It was obvious that he thought this was a good idea, and the more he thought it was a good idea, the more it meant it probably wasn't. But I was still curious.

And suddenly words were coming out of me. "Come on, Tasha, we been cool all this time, and we've never asked you about the parties. We'll be on our best behavior. We'll slide in, scope it out, then slide out. We won't eat nothing, drink nothing, we won't even touch nothing! I swear." I could hardly believe I said it, but I knew it was the best thing to say to get her to come around.

Tasha stood there for a second. She looked from Noodles to me, and then she looked at the ground. Then at the sky. Then she turned around so that her back was facing us. Then she whipped back around and slapped both hands on her hips.

"Under one condition," she said. Her lips started to turn up to a smirk, and then to a full smile. Whatever she was about to say, she thought it was pretty funny. "You gotta bring Needles."

"WHAT?" Noodles shouted.

Needles smiled. "I'll go," he said, soft but loud enough for us to hear.

"No way!" Noodles snapped at Needles. "Tasha, you crazy?"

Needles's smile sank, and he went back to his knitting. I could tell that one stung.

"Wait, wait," I started. "So you saying that we can come if Needles is with us?"

"Yep. He has to be there."

"Why?" Noodles whined.

"Because I like him. And of the three of you, he's the most responsible," she joked. Well, she didn't really joke. She meant that. But she smiled when she said it.

I knew that this had nothing to do with Tasha liking Needles, or wanting him there. She was banking on us backing down, because she figured there was no way we would show up to a MoMo party with Needles. I wanted to look cool, and Noodles definitely wanted to look cool, and Tasha knew we would think we wouldn't look as cool showing up with Needles. It's messed up, but it's true. This was about her tricking us into not coming. Luckily, Doris taught me to always stay a step ahead.

"Cool. We'll be there," I said, calling her bluff.

I could feel Noodles on me, glaring at me hard enough to cave in my chest. I could feel Needles as well, wanting to cheese, but trying hard not to.

Tasha stared me down. She didn't think I meant it. Either that, or she was sure that Noodles wouldn't allow it, or I would lose my nuts and steer clear of trouble. And that would've normally been the case, but this was a pretty big deal. This was a MoMo party.

"When is it?" I asked. Noodles had totally backed out of the conversation at this point. I could smell his panic.

"Wednesday night. Eight, until. He likes to start early."

"Wednesday night?" I asked. I couldn't believe it was on a Wednesday. Who has parties on Wednesdays? They're supposed to be on weekends. "No sweat," I said, trying to recover.

Tasha stood there with "Are you serious?" smeared across her face. I guess she was waiting for me to yell "Sike!" and then we'd all laugh about it. But I didn't. Once she realized I wasn't going to back down, she just walked away. No goodbye, no see y'all later, no nothing. She just left, almost as if she was in some sort of trance—a she-just-couldn't-believe I-on-behalf-of-the-three-of-us-agreed-to-bring-Needles-to-a-MoMo-party trance.

★ 5 ★

Huge. Major. Insane. Supreme. Mega. Ultra.

"Bro, this is ginormous! Next-level large!" I said as soon as Tasha was far enough away, trying to use every word I could think of to convince Noodles that we had made the right decision. "I'm talking, freakin' Juggernaut!"

Noodles looked at me crazy. I figured throwing in a comic book character was worth a shot. I almost wanted to say, "Come on, bro, the X-Men would do it," but I knew that would be pushing it. I was trying anything to convince him of how great this was—a MoMo party, and all we had to do was bring Needles. Nothing to it.

"What if he starts spazzing?" Noodles asked, giving me a dark look. We were still sitting on the stoop. Well, this was uncomfortable—Needles was sitting right there! Second step from the top. A few inches away from us.

"I won't," Needles said lightly. Thankfully, he seemed totally unfazed.

"How you know you won't? You don't even know that," Noodles said, cold. Real cold.

"Because I won't. I just know, man." He looked over at me, his eyes bugging, begging me to bail him out. "Ali . . ."

"Because it's a party, Nood. Everybody will be partying and dancing and drinking," I cut in. "Ain't nobody gonna be worried about none of us. Period."

Noodles clearly wanted to talk to me alone about the whole situation, so he made up an excuse to go inside, telling Needles that we were just going up to their apartment to get something to drink, while giving me the signal to play along.

"Yeah, man, you want me to bring you something out? It's hot," I said, trying to act normal.

Needles said he was fine, and then I realized that he had to have known we were lying because, long as I've known them, they've never had anything to drink in their house. Never. Except water. New York City's finest. And Needles knows Noodles don't drink water.

Their place was nothing like mine. There was no Jazz yapping on the phone to her girlfriends, convincing them not to have crushes on her older brother—me. No Doris at the kitchen sink covered in hard work. No pictures of old times and kids, bucktoothed cheesing. No boxing trophies (just for participating in Malloy's training, not for actually fighting and winning). None of that. Noodles and Needles's apartment was cold. Not cold like the temperature cold, but cold like the feeling cold. Like there was no life there. Like there was just a sad vibe all around. The air was thick and musty.

It was hard to breathe in there sometimes, especially on a hot day like that one. The paint was peeling off the wall. It kinda reminded me of a snake shedding its skin, but there wasn't nothing new underneath.

Whenever I came over, we never went to their room. We just stayed in the front and sat at an old card table they had set up in the middle of the living room. It was just big enough to fit a small TV on it and a few plates, but their apartment didn't exactly seem like a "sit at the table and eat" kind of place. The TV was connected to an orange extension cord that was plugged in on the other side of the room. It was on when we came in. A snowy Channel 1 News talked about something bad that they were being overdramatic about.

I've only seen Noodles and Needles's mother a few times. I don't really know what to say about her—plus, I don't like talking about folks' moms. All I know is, most of the time she's not there.

I assumed she was gone as usual, but then I started smelling smoke coming from the back.

"Roland, somebody here with you?" Her voice, rough but still sweet, came down the hall. It's always weird when I hear anyone call Noodles by his government name, Roland.

"Yeah, it's just Ali," Noodles mumbled, shaking his head.

"Oh. Hi, Ali."

"Hi, Ms. Janice." She made me call her Ms. Janice. Actually, she'd prefer just Janice, but I always called her "Ms." just because you never know when Doris might pop up, and she ain't play calling elders just by their first names. Ms. Janice didn't seem to mind the "Ms." as long as I didn't call her Ms. James, which was her last name, or "ma'am."

"Roland, come close my door," she said, coughing. Noodles disappeared into the smoky hallway. I peeked around the corner. I could see a mattress on the floor and brown skin, but I couldn't make out what part of her body it was. Then I sat down on a fold-up chair with the plastic torn off the seat part, so the yellow foam stuffing was out. The foam had gotten pretty nasty from all the butts that had sat on it.

I heard Noodles's mother's bedroom door click shut. Then I heard another door open. Noodles was digging around for something. A few seconds later I heard that door shut, and Noodles reappeared from the hallway. I don't even know how he could breathe with all the smoke back there, but I guess he was just used to it. He was holding a loose page of a comic book. Just like the first day I'd seen him. The colors were bright, and the edges were raggedy from the tear. He sat down on the other chair and pulled up to the card table. Then Noodles reached over and turned the TV off.

"What's that one?" I asked, nodding at the comic.

"Spawn," he said, all serious. "Black superhero. Don't take no BS."

He dug down in his pocket and wiggled out the mini notepad. He flipped through the sketched pages until he found where he had tucked another folded-up comic book page. He took the tightly folded rectangle from the notepad and set it on the table, and judging by the little bits of cartoony blue and gray, it looked like Batman, but I wasn't sure. Then he started to fold up the Spawn comic as a replacement.

"Yo, so about Needles," he reminded me. "Are you crazy? I just don't think it's a good look, man. You know how he is." We plucked the folded Batman square back and forth—a lazy game of table football.

"He'll be fine, Nood. He's not dumb. The syndrome don't mean he's nuts. Just different, but not really even that much different." I couldn't figure out a better way to explain it.

Noodles put one hand on top of his head. He scratched it only when he was about to speak.

"I guess you're right." He dug his fingers into his scalp and conceded. "And it is a big deal. A MoMo party." His turn to pluck.

"Right. It'll be good for him too," I said, still trying to justify Needles coming with us. But I really did believe that he'd be fine and that it was no big deal. Needles had his yarn, so he won't be shouting nothing, and even if he did, the music would be so loud, no one would even care. Not to mention, Needles is such a shy dude, I figured he'd most likely find a corner to sit in and knit while Noodles and I scope the scene.

"Yeah, maybe you right."

"Needles might find him a pretty lady. Who knows?"

"To do what with, knit?"

"To knit for. And to kick raps about!"

We both laughed.

"So we in?"

Noodles nodded while still scratching his head. "Yeah, we in."

The fridge buzzed like there was a beehive in the freezer. And something was clicking. Not sure what. Then there was a bunch of horn honking coming from right in front of the house. Noodles and I got up to see what the fuss was, but before we could get to the window, Ms. Janice came dashing from the back, tugging at her shirt and buttoning her skin-tight pants. She carried a purse in one hand and an overnight duffel bag in the other.

"Aight, Roland, I'm off to work," she said, scrambling around. She looked good but not good for a young woman, if that makes sense. "See y'all tomorrow."

Noodles didn't say nothing.

"Bye, Ms. Janice," I said to make it less awkward.

Her heels clicked on the wooden hall floor, out the door, and down the steps.

Me and Noodles watched out the window as she ran down the stoop, passed Needles, and into the black cab. She didn't even acknowledge him. I didn't say nothing. I never asked what work she was going to do because it was none of my business, and honestly, whatever it was, Noodles didn't seem like he liked it, which means he probably wouldn't want to talk about it.

Once the cab pulled off, we went back downstairs.

"Yo, Needles," Noodles said in his usual gruff tone as soon as we got to the stoop, "you partying with us or what?"

Good enough, I thought. Actually, I was pretty psyched

because since Noodles asked, that meant he was now totally into the whole idea.

Needles smiled, and ticked a little, his left arm jerking just enough for the yarn to slip off the needle. "Sure, guys, I'm down"—he paused, then smiled and continued—"like the ground, from here to downtown." Then he let out an "Ohhhhhhhh!" He was his own biggest fan.

I felt good. I felt like, somehow, we all were winning.

Now came the next problem. The party was only three days away, and the trickiest part about it was figuring out what we were going to wear, how we were going to look. I mean, it's not like we're girls or nothin', primping in front of the mirror for hours, but like I said, this was a big deal.

The issue was, Needles was sixteen, almost seventeen, and Noodles and I was fifteen going on sixteen. But MoMo was twenty going on thirty; his party was going to be jam-packed with a bunch of folks who broke out their best fits to show off. People were probably going to rent cars and spend a few hundred dollars on a slick pair of shoes. Every dude was going to have a haircut so fresh that he was still going to smell like the oil and the spray the barber always puts on your head afterward, to give it that shine and make the waves pop out. It was going to be quite a sight, and we couldn't be the only three lames in there looking like we still played with blocks.

First on the agenda: haircuts.

The next day, Monday, I went to do some work over at Malloy's early in the morning, wiping down all the boxing equipment, taking out the trash, and doing whatever other little odd jobs he needed me to do, since he wouldn't let me do it the day before. It usually only took about an hour, and he always gave me twenty dollars for it. Twenty bucks, three times a week, can add up, and I wish I would've done a better job at saving some of it, because then I'd be able to at least buy some fresh kicks for the party. But who knew we would end up going to a MoMo party? Plus, I always used some of my cash to help out around the house, just to take some of the load off Doris.

I came bopping down the block, swinging a bodega bag. Needles and Noodles were sitting on the stoop, waiting for me. We would just pool all of our money and see how much we had and what we could afford. We knew we wouldn't have enough for fly outfits, but at least we might be able to get haircuts.

I dug in the black bag and pulled out a greasy brown paper one. Then I wiggled a golden beef patty out and broke a piece off. I passed the patty to Needles, who cracked off a corner and then passed the rest to his brother.

"How much you got," Noodles said, sucking in his breath—the patty was hot!

"I got eleven bucks," I said. I took my money and held it in my hand like it was a wad. "Here's eight of it, and the rest of it is in change." I patted my pocket so they could hear the jingle.

"Okay, cool," Noodles gave his approval. "You?" He turned and looked at Needles, who was sitting on the second step from the top as usual. Needles put the yarn down and wiggled his hand into his left pocket. He pulled out a few dollars.

"Here you go," Needles said, happily handing it over.

"One, two, three, four. Four bucks." Noodles looked disappointed. "That's it?"

"Yeah, that's it," Needles said, now looking bummed.

Noodles was always coming down on Needles, and it was really starting to piss me off.

"Man, how much you got?" I said.

Noodles looked at me strange.

"I could probably get us a couple of bucks. I just gotta wait for Ma to get back from work," he said, which meant he had nothing.

"So you got nothing? Not one dollar? Not a quarter? Not a penny? Even bums got pennies!" I knew this would make him angry, and I didn't care. I looked up at Needles and he was giggling. That's all I cared about. "Well, fifteen bucks ain't gonna be enough for all three of us to get cut," I said.

"Welp, sorry, Needles." Noodles looked at his brother and shrugged his shoulders.

"Naw, naw, he can get one. I was just gonna get a shape-up, but I can pass." My hair was in braids. I knew that I could get away with not having a fresh shape-up easier than they could get away with not chopping that Sunday dinner off the tops of their heads. "I'll just get Jazz to braid me up fresh. No biggie," I added.

"Fifteen still ain't enough to get both of us cut, man."

"Brother will hook it up. He'll look out because he likes Needles. Should be fine."

I really wasn't sure if Brother would look out for Needles, but I knew he probably would just because everyone in our neighborhood kind of looked out for him, as long as he wasn't bugging out.

We started heading up the block toward Brother's. Once we got halfway up the street, we realized Needles wasn't behind us. He was still sitting on the stoop. He just wasn't used to ever coming anywhere with us, I guess. It was like his mind had gotten used to us, and everyone, leaving him right there on that stoop, second step from the top. We called out to him, and he looked kind of startled.

"Come on, man!" Noodles shouted, waving his arm.

Needles scrambled to gather his stuff, his yarn and needles, and ran to catch up.

We walked up Fulton like three cool dudes, one of which was holding yarn. For some reason this particular day Fulton Street felt like Broadway, or Fifth Ave, one of those kind of streets. Not because anything on the street was different, because it wasn't. Same old hood shops, and hustlers on the corner. People on pay phones and the smell of burnt halal meat and dog mess. No white people. At least not many. So it wasn't actually like Broadway or Fifth Ave, but in my mind it just felt like we were walking high and mighty like I guessed they did on those streets. Like we were going to do something very important. Get haircuts for a very special event we'd been invited to. An exclusive night at Chateau MoMo.

Once we got to Brother's Barbershop and Pet Store, there was a blue and white sign on the door. SORRY WE'RE CLOSED. Closed? Closed? How?

I checked the hours on the sign.

"He's closed Mondays," I said.

Noodles put his forehead against the glass door and peered in. Darkness.

"You gotta be kidding me. What about the pet store? Brother gotta be in there. People need pet stuff on Mondays, don't they?"

"Guess not." I stared at the sign as if trying to change it from closed to open. Needles leaned against the wall, quiet.

"Yeah, all barbershops, for the most part, are closed on Mondays, young fellas." A familiar voice came from behind us. I looked in the glass before turning around. I could see the reflection and knew exactly who it was.

It was this guy named Kendall who lived all the way down at the end of our block. Everyone called him Black. I'm pretty sure he was twenty-something. Definitely not over thirty. He was known for being a hustler but not your typical hustler. His hustle was that he could do a whole bunch of stuff pretty good. He wasn't great at anything, though. Just pretty good. My mother says he's a jackass of all trades, and a master of none. He would hang out on Fulton, and whatever stores were closed, he would lurk around and wait for customers to show up and be disappointed about the store not being open. Then he would offer his services. So if a law office wasn't open on Sundays, Black would just pop up and say he could represent someone in court. Or if a restaurant was closed, he'd appear out of nowhere and offer to make people lunch for half the price. I guess it was our day.

"But whatever you need done, I'm sure I could hook you right up. And for cheap, too."

Noodles looked at him from head to toe. Then looked at me. I knew I wasn't getting a haircut either way, because I have braids, so it didn't matter too much to me. And even if Black said he'd braid it, I would've said no, just because nobody does my hair but Jazz. She does it the best, and it's free. I gave Noodles the "why not" face. I mean, we were in a jam. What other options did we have? Sure, we could wait until the next day, but we figured all the barbershops on this side of Brooklyn would be slammed with all the other guys trying to get fresh for MoMo's party, plus barbershops are just generally pretty busy places in our neighborhood. The black man's country club, as they say.

"Aight, man," Noodles said to Black. He put his tough face on. "What you talking?"

Black smiled a hustler's smile. "What you need?"

"Me and him, caesars." Noodles pointed over to Needles, who was still leaning against the wall.

Black looked at Needles, and you could tell he recognized him from the neighborhood.

"Oh, cool," Black said. He took a second to think of a price. It looked like he was punching a calculator in his head. He was counting his fingers, too. It was all very stupid. He knew what he wanted to charge, he was just stalling to make it seem like he was cutting them some kind of deal.

"Just give me ten and we square," he said.

Noodles looked over at me. I gave the same face I gave him before. Why not? I mean, the truth is, I had seen Black's work. Not his barber skills, but I saw him fix Mr. Malloy's gate down the block, and he patched a leak in my house one time, for Doris. And he brought me and Jazz bootleg movies to watch. Pretty good. Good enough. Oh, and he put braid extensions in some girl's hair once. I can't remember who, but I remember them looking pretty good, and her bragging about only paying him thirty bucks or something like that. He had proven to be a decent knockoff guy.

In order to get the haircuts, though, we had to go back to Black's apartment. None of us felt like walking back to the block, but luckily, Black had a car. A cab. I guess another of his hustles. We jumped in the backseat and headed back down Fulton.

Black's place was interesting. He lived alone, which was cool and unexpected. I don't know why, but I always thought he lived with his mother. I guess all his hustles were paying off. The walls were painted a cool light blue, and the room seemed brighter than it really was. The living room was the first room you walk into. He had a supernice couch and table in there, and even had a flat-screen TV. A sweet one. They're all sweet, but his was sweet. Black actually had pretty good taste, from what I could tell.

"Come right through here, gents," he said while leading us toward the back of the apartment.

You know how when you see movies where people have attics in their houses, and that's where they keep all their junk, and sometimes scary things go on up there? That's how this back room was in Black's house. He had welding masks, paintbrushes and empty paint cans, a barbecue grill, a chainsaw, curling irons, a flute, blades from a ceiling fan, old TVs with the wires coming out the back, a mannequin, high-heel shoes, and who the hell knows what else. I had no clue why he brought us back to this room until I looked in the corner. A barber chair.

"Are you serious?" Noodles barked.

"What?" Black seemed confused.

"Why do you have all this crap?"

"This is my office. This is what put that flat screen out there, and this is what's gonna get you and him a haircut for cheap," Black boasted.

There was nothing anyone could say after that.

Black cleared some space around the barber chair. There was a black box on the seat. He opened it and began pulling out his clippers and his smock, and the oils and sprays and all that. He had the whole setup. If you didn't know better, you'd have thought Black actually went to school for this. He sprayed the clippers down to clean them and then stood behind the chair.

"So, who's first?"

"Needles," Noodles said with no hesitation. Somehow I knew that was coming.

"Yeah, I'll go first. I don't care," Needles said.

Needles, yarn in hand, stepped over the mess to get to the chair. He plopped down, and I could tell he was happy. He didn't smile or anything, but I could just tell. It was his eyes. It was always his eyes. They were beaming. Black took the smock and waved it over Needles to cover him, tying it around his neck.

"Y'all can have a seat over there," Black said, pointing to an old church pew. What the? I didn't even want to know what he was doing with that. Clippers on. The motor inside was buzzing at the exact same level as the fridge in Noodles and Needles's house. Black started with the back, moving the clippers up Needles's neck in sweeping motions like he was painting. He looked pretty pro.

Still, I had to warn him. "Black, be careful," I said. "Needles sometimes has a tick. Don't want you to put a bald spot in his head. That wouldn't be cool."

"Gotcha," he said. "Trust me, I've cut enough babies to know how to handle that kind of stuff."

"Needles ain't no baby," Noodles said, tough. I understood why he said it, but I think he misunderstood what Black was saying. Black didn't respond. Noodles just smirked.

"I'll try not to budge, Black," Needles said.

"You aight, man, no worries. I gotcha."

The clippers buzzed and buzzed, and hair fell from Needles's head like ash. Like thick black snow. Black told us about how he used to watch Brother cut when he was younger. How he would sit with his mom waiting for a cut, watching everything Brother would do with the clippers.

How he would hold them when he was cutting, and even how he would whisper to himself, "Against the grain," or "Go with the grain." I never knew what Brother was saying, but he's always mumbling something. I guess that's what it was. Against the grain. Or go with the grain. Black said that's pretty much how he learned everything he knew. He learned to braid hair from watching his mom get hers braided. He learned to fix things by watching his mother's boyfriend. He learned to cook by watching his mother in the kitchen. Then he told us how he didn't really do well in school because no one was ever showing him anything, so he couldn't quite understand most of the subjects. He said teachers were just talking. Not showing. And he was a show-don't-tell kind of guy. Black said he probably could've been a scientist or a doctor or a lawyer if his teachers had got that he was different. I agreed. He probably could've been. I told him that I bet he could be a teacher, though. He laughed.

Right when he was finishing up Needles's haircut, there was a clicking at the front door. Someone was coming in. We could hear the door swing open and tap against the wall. Then close. Lock. The click-clacking on the floor made it clear that it was a woman. She peeked into the back room and tapped on the wall to get Black's attention.

"Hey, babe, what you got goin' on in here?"

"Not much. Just cutting these boys' hair." Black cut the clippers off and stretched out to give her a kiss. "Fellas, this is my girl, Kim."

Kim smiled. "Hey, guys." She shook all of our hands,

classy. "Kenny, I'm gonna be out here on the couch. Gonna try to catch a quick nap before work."

"Okay, we'll keep it down."

Kim wasn't bad to look at. She was tall and slim but not skinny. She had super white teeth and she wore glasses, which I liked. From that short interaction, she seemed so sweet, which made her look even better. It was sort of amazing that a girl like her was with Black. Not that he was a bad-looking guy, but he was Black: jackass of all trades, master of none. But I was learning as we were talking that he wasn't so bad. Still, I couldn't believe she was Black's girl. Pretty good.

Black didn't really say too much about Kim when she left, just brushed off Needles's neck and forehead, then sprayed the stuff on his head to make sure it had that shine. He pulled a hand mirror out of the black box and held in front of Needles's face. Needles smiled big. I did too. I looked over at Noodles. He smiled too. I have to say, the haircut was fresh.

"Next," Black said while taking the smock off Needles and snapping it in the air. Hair went flying and slowly falling to the tops of everything on the floor. Noodles jumped up, now excited since he'd seen that Black actually was a decent barber.

Black started from the back again, cutting upward toward the top of Noodles's head. What Black said about watching Brother cut became obvious, because while he was cutting Noodles, I realized that he cut exactly like Brother did. His posture. His facial expressions. His movements. Brother, Brother, Brother.

After he finished, he held the hand mirror in front of Noodles. Noodles looked and looked, and looked some more. He turned his head to the left and to the right. I couldn't understand what he was looking for. His cut looked crisp. His hairline looked perfect, and in the hood, that's a big deal. That's like a fresh pair of shoes.

Noodles kept analyzing it, and for some reason, for some strange reason, I just knew what was about to go down.

Noodles twisted his face. "Yo, man, what's this?"

Black was dusting off his clippers. He came around to the front of the chair.

"What's what?"

"This." Noodles took his hand and traced his hairline. "It's crooked."

Black looked concerned. He knew he had done a good job, and I did too.

"Where?"

"Are you blind? Here!" Noodles ran his finger along his perfectly straight hairline again.

"It ain't crooked, man," Black said, looking as hard as he could.

"Yeah, man, it don't look crooked to me, either," I said, trying to squash this before it got too far.

"Me either," said Needles.

"What? Man, this thing is crooked! Look like you shaped me up with your eyes closed. Like you drunk. Better yet, like you gotta syndrome!" Noodles jumped up from the chair and snatched the smock off. I already knew what he was doing. He was pulling the same crap he always pulls. I stood up to make sure he didn't try to do nothing crazy, like swing on Black, though I didn't really think he would go that far.

"I ain't paying for this crap!" Noodles said. "You butchered me!" Then he looked at me and howled, "He butchered me, Ali! I can't go to the party like this!"

"Calm down, Nood," I said in my calmest voice.

Black picked the smock up off the floor. "I don't know what your deal is, man, but that's a mean cut. And you owe me ten bucks." He laid the smock on the back of the chair. He was moving in such a relaxed way that it kind of scared me. He didn't seem put off by any of this. That made me believe that he knew something we didn't know. Like, nobody was leaving until he got his money. Like, in all this junk in this room, there might've also been a gun.

"Yeah, man, just pay him his money," I pleaded with Noodles. "Just give it to him."

"I ain't giving him ten bucks! Maybe five for Needles, but he ain't cut me right! Mine is messed up!"

I glared at him. Why'd he have to pull this now? I mean, he had money—me and Needles's money. He just was trying to get over on Black and get something for nothing. But I knew for sure, Noodles wasn't gonna win this one.

"Listen," Black said, taking a step toward him, "I'm not playing with you. Ten bucks, homie."

"You not playing with me? You not playing with me?" Noodles started, his voice rising to another level each time he said it. "I'm not playing with you!" He balled his fists up tight, but I knew he really didn't want no parts of Black.

I grabbed Noodles and started pulling him back. Kim came into the room, and after some more yelling from Noodles, she asked us to leave. Noodles took five of the dollars he had, five of our dollars, balled them up, and threw them at Black. Black bit down on his jaw, trying his best to hold in the butt-whooping he surely had ready for Noodles. Needles, shaking his head, ran over and picked the dollars up and handed them to Black. I realized he wasn't surprised at Noodles's performance either, and was just as prepared for it as I was. I pulled an extra five from my pocket and dropped it on the church pew while yanking Noodles out of the room.

It's funny. Another one of my mother's rules was to never let anyone know what you're holding. Not even your friends. I had more than eight dollars in cash. But somehow I knew it would be a bad idea to let Noodles know that. I knew I would have to have a reserve messing around with him. And I'm glad I did.

I apologized to Kim on the way out, and asked her to please apologize to Black on behalf of the three of us. I also told her to make sure he got the extra five I left on the pew for him. She was upset, but still sweet enough to smile at me while closing the door.

"Yo, what's your deal, Noodles?" I laid into him as soon as we hit the sidewalk. I was mad, and this time I wanted him to know it. "Why do you insist on being such a jerk, man?"

"Whatever, Ali. I just ain't feel like paying that fool. Figured we could use that money for something else," Noodles said proudly.

I shook my head in disgust. "Trippin'."

"I'm trippin'? What about you, Mr. Moneybags? You was holding out."

"And you wasn't holding at all, so who are you to count my coins, man?" I almost snapped on him, but I caught myself. "Yo, just forget it. The haircuts are fresh. That's all that matters."

That's all that mattered. But I was starting to understand what my mother said about getting tired of bailing people out. I wasn't ready to quit on my homeboy yet, but he was pushing me, and pushing hard.

★ 6 ★

Doris always says that the worst thing ever is a man dressed up in a sharp suit, wearing dirty shoes. And since we don't wear no suits, that's like saying the worst thing is a dude with a fresh haircut, wearing a wack outfit, which we agreed could not be us. Not for a MoMo party. So we sat around knocking our heads together, trying to figure out a way to get clothes. Good clothes. A fresh white tee right out of a three-pack wouldn't cut it. We needed something with some flash to it. Something with a name so hard to pronounce that people don't even try. The kind of clothes that would cost more money than any of us had, or ever had. There was no way for us to get it unless we did something crazy, which I wasn't down for. Noodles, on the other hand, as usual, was all about pulling a caper.

"We need money to get these clothes." Noodles sat in my living room drinking a soda, stating the obvious. Needles stayed outside on the stoop. I told him to come in, but I guess he didn't want to, and I was starting to get it. I think he felt safe on the stoop. I couldn't blame him. His brother knew how to make things real unsafe, real quick.

"That's all, man. Money. Lots of it," he continued. I sat at the window. Didn't really have much to say to Noodles. I was still upset about what went down at Black's. I was trying to move past it, but it was really bugging me. Plus, he'd jumped all over Needles for picking the money up off the floor and giving it to Black.

"You ain't no dog! You don't gotta pick nothing up off the floor, stupid!" he said, slapping Needles in the back of the head.

"What you gotta hit me for?" Needles yelped. He rubbed the back of his head. "And I ain't stupid either," he said.

"Tell him again, bro," I said, backing Needles up.

"Yeah, whatever," Noodles said. He turned to me. "Stay out of this."

I should've said, "Hit him again, Noodles, and I'll show you what Black should've done to you." But I didn't. For some reason I just didn't feel like I had the right to step that far into family business, because family business is family business.

Now Noodles tapped the soda can on the kitchen table.

"Man, we can't rob no bank, but we could jack a bodega, easy."

Just the thought of robbing a corner store made me cringe, especially knowing all the drama it caused my family when my father did it. But I didn't say nothing.

"Or go into the city where the fancy folks live with their little dogs, and snatch a purse. Probably be straight just from one bag. Take whatever cash is in it, and if it's not enough, we could sell the bag and get Needles some fly clothes too."

Nothing.

"Or we could just take Needles to a church and do the whole, my brother is sick with a syndrome and we don't have no clothes, please help, bit."

Nothing.

"Naw, that's probably not a good one, because they won't give us money, they'd probably give us clothes. Church clothes. And I ain't wearing that mess to the party. Corduroys and whatnot."

I still said nothing. He went on and on about different ways to steal money from this person and that person. How we could somehow cheat and either make a fistful of cash or a closet full of clothes suddenly appear. He even suggested that I ask my mother to somehow "get" some stuff from the store she works at, as if Doris was just going to say, "Of course I'll get you and your little knucklehead friend a boatload of expensive clothes" without asking what we needed the clothes for. Or without yelling my head off for asking her something so ridiculous.

As Noodles made suggestion after suggestion, I looked out at Needles, sitting on the stoop, weaving the black yarn in and out with the needles just like my mother taught him. I could see that something had started to form. Something was being made, and even if it wasn't anything specific, it was something, and I thought that was pretty cool. He was making progress. You could tell he was concentrating on every stitch and loving every moment while this black, messy glob of together-yarn was being created. And suddenly, without warning, he jerked. His left arm shot out, sort of like a toy with a spring-loaded karate chop. And just like that, the messy glob of together-yarn came loose again.

"Or we could just go see Dog and ask him to put us down for a trial run, see how good we can make a flip." Noodles was still tossing out ridiculous ideas. Ideas like going to see Dog, the block's dope boy, and asking him if we could sell for him. At that point it became pretty clear that Noodles was going crazy. He was willing to risk his life over an outfit for this party. "You hear me?" he asked.

I heard him, but I definitely wasn't listening.

"Yeah, I hear you," I said, straight and to the point.

"So, what you think about any of those ideas?" Noodles was finishing off his soda. He turned the can up to his mouth and took the last few swallows. Burp. Then he put the can on the table, broke the aluminum tab thing, the thing you open it with, off the top, and popped it in his mouth like it was candy.

"I think they're terrible," I said.

Noodles's eyes looked like they were ready to fall out his face.

"You got something better, genius? Oh, I mean, money-bags," he asked, all huff and puff. If he was a girl, he would've rolled his eyes. And his neck.

The aluminum tab in his mouth made it sound like he had a mouthful of loose teeth. I could tell he was trying hard not to drool when he was talking.

"Let me ask you something," I said. "Why you so mean to Needles?"

I don't know where it came from, but it came. For some reason I just couldn't hold it in no more.

Noodles squinted his eyes like he didn't know what I was talking about. "What?" he said in his usual grouchy tone.

"You heard me. Why are you always so mean to your brother? He's your brother."

Noodles took the tab from his mouth and dropped it into the empty can. He then grabbed the can and crushed it between his hands.

"You don't know what you talkin' about, Ali."

"Just answer the question, Nood. You smack him around and give him all kind of flack for nothing. You shut him down every time he says something. It's ridiculous. And all these folks around here don't wanna say nothing, 'cause they not trying to be bothered with all your mess." I could feel my voice starting to get a little more intense. "I know you, the real you, and I don't care about your mess, so now I'm calling you out on it." I wanted to say that I knew Noodles the comic book nerd.

"Ali, I think you crossing the line," Noodles said, as if he was trying to say I better chill before he does something.

It's not really like me to go off, but I couldn't stop.

"Seems like all you do is give him hell for no reason, and he just takes it!"

"You don't know nothing, Ali! You don't know what me and Needles got going on! You don't know what it's like to have a brother with a syndrome! Jazz ain't got no syndrome! So, who are you? Who are you to sit here and tell me how to deal with my brother?"

Noodles was now standing up. And so was I. His chest was all puffed up like he was seconds away from throwing himself at me. Let him.

"Yeah, you right, Noodles. I don't know what it's like to have a brother with a syndrome, but you the only person around here who treats Needles different. You ever notice that? You the only one! The rest of the hood treats him like he don't have a syndrome at all. You the one who keeps treating him like he got some kind of handicap or something! Maybe you got the problem!"

"Oh yeah? Maybe I got a problem? Maybe I do! Maybe I got a problem with you not minding your business! And maybe we should solve this problem right now, Ali! What you think? You wanna solve it?"

Noodles was in my face now. His hands clenched tight. I still wasn't scared because I could look in his eyes and see he wasn't trying to fight me. My mother always said the eyes say a lot, and his eyes weren't saying nothing about fighting. They were saying something totally different. Something sad. He looked like he was about to cry. I could tell I had hit a soft spot, but I couldn't figure out how to cool the situation without seeming like I was backing down from a fight. I needed Noodles to know that I meant business as much as he did, and that he couldn't intimidate me with all his yapping. But I did not want to fight him in my mother's kitchen. I mean, he's my friend, plus Doris would be pissed. I was hoping Jazz would magically appear from the back with a funny joke, but she was staying at a friend's house. Then I hoped Mom would come home from her first job early. Anything to get him to back up off me without me having to tell him to.

We stood there chest to chest for a second, Noodles egging me on, telling me to do something and solve the problem. Then the door clicked. It clicked again. Someone was trying to get in. It clicked again, and then it opened. Noodles backed up as a man stumbled awkwardly into the apartment.

I looked closely to see who it was, one hand close enough to the kitchen knives to pull one easily, just in case. Then I recognized him.

"Dad?" I said.

The man, my father, finally got his balance and straightened up.

"Ali, wassup, man," he said.

I walked over to him and gave him five and a half hug. Then suddenly he jumped back and threw a quick tap to the ribs, as a test to see if I was any quicker with my hands. I was slow on the block, and he tagged me. It stung a little, but I played it off.

"Too slow, son!" He laughed and palmed the top of my head, wiggling it around. I hated when he did that.

My dad, John, is a regular-looking dude. By that, I mean, there really wasn't anything special about the way he looked. If a cop ever asked me to describe him, it would be hard because there have to be a million men who look just like him. He's dark skinned, brown eyes, low haircut, full beard, earrings in both ears, no tattoos, average height, average weight, average dude. He was dressed in black jeans, a black button-up shirt, and black boots. Everything clean. Not bad for a booster, but nothing special.

"What you doing here?" I asked, confused. Not that I wasn't happy to see him. He just usually gave a heads up just because he didn't really like to stop by without knowing whether or not Doris was home. He usually sent some kind of warning to me. A text message or something.

"Man, I was around here doing some business, so I figured I'd pop in. Your mother ain't here, is she?" he asked, peeking around.

"Naw, she ain't here."

"Jazz?"

"Nope. She ain't here either."

"Oh. Okay." I could tell he was bummed about not catching Jazz home. She was definitely a daddy's girl, and he was definitely a daughter's dad. He looked over at Noodles. "Wassup, boy," he said, slapping Noodles in the chest playfully.

Noodles pretended like it didn't sting. "Wassup, John."

It had slipped my mind that Noodles and I were seconds away from ripping each other's heads off before John came busting in. John had no idea that he was right on time.

"Not much. Ain't seen you in a minute, Noodles. Getting grown, ain't ya?"

"Trying to."

"How's your brother?"

"Good. Sitting outside on the stoop."

"I thought that was him. Wasn't sure."

Probably because he was knitting.

"Yeah."

Then there was sort of an awkwardness that started filling up the space between us all, and I could tell that John knew something was up. But before he asked why we were acting weird, something else important dawned on me.

"Dad," I started while pulling out a chair at the table, "I'm glad you came by, actually. I need a favor. Well, we need a favor."

The one thing I know about John is that he's a good guy. And he'll do anything to prove that to his kids. He always tells me and Jazz to call him if we need anything, but we never call, only because we never really need anything. Mom pretty much takes care of everything, and what she doesn't, Jazz and I take care of ourselves. But I needed him now.

"Okay, wassup?" he said, smiling. It was like he was excited to even be asked.

"Well, we need clothes. And I know what you do for money, so I figured you might have some."

I didn't know how else to say it. I looked at Noodles. I could tell he wasn't expecting me to say that, but he caught on and fell in line quick.

"Clothes?"

"Yep, clothes," I said. Noodles nodded his head in agreement, finally taking a seat next to me. Friends again.

"What kind of clothes?" John was now sitting on the arm of the couch, something that Doris would have his head for if she caught him. He looked comfortable. Like he lived here.

"I don't know, the best kind?" I said.

John laughed. Hard. I mean, keeled over and slapped his knee laughing. I wasn't sure if I actually said something funny, or if he just found Noodles and me asking for nice clothes so outrageous that laughter was the only possible response.

"The best kind? The best kind? I see," he said, brushing his beard down with the palm of his hand. "So let's just air it out, Ali. Where you going?" Parents always know. Even parents who only halfway parent.

"A party." Figured I might as well just cut to the chase.

"Where?"

"You know MoMo?" I knew he knew MoMo. He probably remembered when MoMo was born.

John smiled. "Your mother know?"

I didn't say anything.

"Your mother know, Ali?" John asked again. It's funny. He was just enough of a father for it to matter. He wasn't really there, but he also wasn't a deadbeat. Sometimes it got confusing.

"No," I answered honestly. I knew Noodles couldn't believe I was telling my father the truth, when I could have easily just said that Doris knew. It's not like John would've checked because John and Doris don't really talk. At least not much. But I don't lie too well. So I didn't lie. Plus, John's a pretty cool guy.

My dad smiled again. "So you sneaking?" I could tell by the way he asked that he was surprised. He knew I wasn't really the sneaky type. That was more his deal. I couldn't tell if he was concerned or proud.

I looked at the floor. "Yeah, but it's kind of a big deal, man. We got invited, and nobody gets invited to these parties."

"Nobody y'all's age," he shot back. He got up from the couch and walked over to where we were sitting. "But I remember what it was like being fifteen. I do. So here's what we'll do. We'll trade."

Huh? "What for what?"

"Clothes for a couple of text messages."

"What you mean?"

"I mean, I'll give you the clothes. But your scrawny ass gotta text me when you get there, and when you make it back home. What time the party start?"

"Eight."

"Aight, so that means you need to be back by eleven. Got it?" He held out his fist.

I almost did a back flip. And I can't even do a back flip, but I almost did one. I was trying to contain the excitement and be cool, and I could tell Noodles was trying just as hard.

"Got it," I said, giving him a pound. "Thanks, man."

"Yeah, thanks, John," Noodles added. "Really appreciate it."

"What you thanking me for?" he asked Noodles.

"Oh," I started, "the clothes are for Noodles, too."

"Aha," he said, startled but still cool with it.

"And Needles."

"Needles too! You trying to break me," he barked. "My own son. Hustling a hustler. Whoever taught you that should be shot!"

He held two fingers to his head and pretended to blow himself away.

★ 7 ★

You know in the movies when the slicksters open up their trench coats and they got gold watches and chains hanging inside? Well, my dad's trench coat was the trunk of his car. It was an old cherry-red Plymouth. It's the same car he used to take my mother on dates in. I know because she always tells me. She said it was a piece of junk back then too, but it was better than the train. Now he didn't have no pretty woman in the passenger seat anymore, but he was still driving it around like he was king of the world, with a kingdom's worth of rags inside.

He popped the trunk. Three suitcases. Each one labeled a different number. One, two, and three. Number one was the biggest.

"Aight, boys. Gotta make this quick before the cops roll up or your mother gets home," John said. Neither of us had to say that the cops would've been ten times better than Doris. "Get close," he said.

He unzipped number one. It was like having a glimpse

into a rich man's closet. Like a glow was coming from all kinds of silk and suede, and funny names that none of us could pronounce, so we knew it was expensive stuff. Noodles reached in and swiped a pretty nice shirt. Gucci. I dug around and found a sharp button-up that was Polo. I handed it to Needles. Then I found myself another shirt, made by one of the fancy brands. I didn't know what it was, but John said it was a good look. Then we grabbed a few pairs of crisp jeans. They were like cardboard. Stiff, raw denim. Probably three hundred bucks in the store.

Then he unzipped number two. Shoes.

"Sorry, guys, sold most of these already," John said. "Give me sizes."

"I'm a ten," I said.

John pulled out a smooth pair of Jordans. Perfect.

"I'm nine and a half," Noodles said.

"What about you, Needles? What size you wear?" John asked.

"Eleven, please," Needles said politely.

John checked the sizes on all of the shoes. He found an eleven for Needles. A pair of boots. Pretty nice ones too. But he couldn't find any nine and a halfs for Noodles.

"All I got left is these in a nine." He held up a pair of Nikes I had never seen before. They looked good to me.

Noodles looked upset.

"They pretty sweet, though," Needles said encouragingly.

"Yeah, dude, they gonna be just a little small, but they'll look good with that shirt. Besides, they better than nothing," I said.

Noodles finally agreed. I mean, it's not like he had a choice.

Then John opened number three. It was stuffed with sunglasses, watches, chains, belts, and all that. We each grabbed a belt but left the jewelry alone. We wanted to be fly but not draw too much attention. A chain of ice cubes didn't seem like a good idea. But the belts really pulled the outfits together.

"Y'all good?" John asked, zipping the bags back up and pulling down the trunk.

"Yeah, we good, man, thanks."

John walked around to the passenger side and opened the door. He moved some things around and threw a blanket into the backseat. When he tossed the blanket, it knocked over a plastic cup that was in the cup holder, which I noticed had a toothbrush in it. A blanket? A toothbrush? What? Wait. Why would he . . . Oh. Ohhh. This could only mean one thing—my dad was living in his car.

My dad was living in his car? Why wouldn't he just come home? Doris would understand. At least I think she would've. Maybe he just didn't want to ask for help, and I could kinda get that. And I knew I couldn't really say nothing about it, because it's just not cool to put people's embarrassing situations on blast. But I felt sad for him. He wasn't some stranger, some bum begging for change. He was my dad.

He dug around a little bit longer until he finally pulled out a hat. A Yankees cap. As he wiggled it out the bag, the bag shifted and I noticed something else. For a moment I couldn't breathe. I looked again—it was the butt of a gun. Sticking up between the console and the driver's seat. It wasn't too obvious, and if you looked fast, it could've passed as the seat-belt thing. I hoped Noodles didn't see it.

At first I was nervous, just because my father wasn't the type to deal with guns. Not after everything he went through before. After he got out of prison that last time, he only dealt with clothes, not robbery or nothing like that. He said he practically swore off guns. But then I thought about the fact that he was living in his car, and maybe he needed to make sure he was safe at night. Made sense, I guess. I looked away from the gun, anywhere away from it, as he walked back over to me and sat the cap on top of my head. He pulled the brim down over my eyes and then stepped back to check me out.

"Now you ready," he said with a fatherly smile. I was caught somewhere between excitement and fear. Part of me wanted to ask him what the gun was for, and another part just wanted to give him a big hug for hooking us up with the clothes. Instead of either of those, I just turned and ducked down a little bit so I could see my reflection in the back window. Fresh.

"When is the party?" John asked.

"Tomorrow night."

John nodded as if he was proud that I was sneaking out and going to a party I was too young to be at.

"Aight, so remember our deal. Text me when you get there and when you get home. You don't, and you'll have me AND Doris to deal with."

The next day I got my braids done. I sat on the floor in the living room while Jazz sat behind me on the couch. She ran a fine-tooth comb through my hair, which she had already unbraided and washed.

"Come on, Jazz," I begged, squinting in pain. "You really don't have to pull that hard." It felt like she was pulling my scalp off.

"You know, I could always just cut it all off for you," she said, tugging on what my mother calls my mane. "Show the world that peanut you got."

"Yeah, and I could box you up," I joked, putting my fists in the air.

"Whatever."

I could feel her grab a handful and separate it into three parts. Then she started braiding. My eyes watered as she wove the hair together, which means she was doing a good job. Whenever she was doing it tight and right, it hurt enough to make me want to cry. Not that I ever did.

I would never tell Jazz this, but I always loved her braiding my hair. Me acting like a punk, her yanking extra hard just to be funny. Even though I was in pain for most of it, I still loved it.

"Jazz?"

"Huh?" she said. I could tell by her voice she was staring at the TV. I don't know why she finds those stupid talk shows so interesting. I could smell the grease. She had a big scoop of it sitting on the back of her hand. My mom does the same thing when she does Jazz's hair. It's for easy access. Dip the comb in it, and take it straight to the scalp. A hood trick. I don't know where Doris learned it. Probably her mom.

"You got a boyfriend?"

I asked her this every time she did my hair, which was about every two weeks. I had to always check because when I was her age, I remember trying to look up skirts and cop feels. And you know . . . I just don't want Jazz to be . . . you know.

"What?" Jazz snapped.

"You heard me."

"Boy, no," she said in her most grown-up voice. "These boys around here too young in the mind."

"Jazz, you eleven."

"Exactly, and they act nine. I ain't got time for that."

"So you telling me, there's no boy around here you like?"

"Nope."

"Not Dante Robinson?"

"Bird Lips? Naw."

"J. J. Mendez?"

"Who?"

"Spanish J. J."

"Oh, you mean Pancake? Face too flat."

"What about Prego across the street?"

"Prego? Are you serious? You know why I call him Prego? 'Cause he waddle like a pregnant woman. He good people, but I can't walk down the block with him looking like he about to lay an egg. Not happening."

I shook my head. She was a trip. I knew that she at least liked these boys as friends, because she had given them all nicknames. I also knew there was somebody she really liked, because her and her little friends were always giggling about something, and boys are usually the main thing little girls giggle about.

I stopped asking and let Jazz zone back into whatever was happening with whoever's baby's mother on the TV. At least I thought she was zoning back in. Apparently, though, she was thinking about the boy she liked, and was itching to tell me.

"Ali?" she said, her voice in eleven-year-old mode again. I liked it like that. Killed me when she sounded too grown-up.

"Yeah," I said, muffled. My head was tilted, and my chin was pressed into my chest. Jazz was combing through the back of my neck. My mother always calls it the kitchen. Seemed like my kitchen was on fire whenever Jazz was cooking.

"I do like somebody," she said, all shy.

"I knew it! Who I gotta kill!" I shouted, laughing.

Jazz pulled the comb from my hair and leaned back on the couch. When I turned around, she had both her hands covering her face.

"Don't tease, Ali! I'm being serious!" She was so embarrassed, and as bad as I wanted to make it worse, as bad as I wanted to come up with a funny nickname on the spot for her, the protector in me kicked in and I couldn't.

"Okay, Jazz. No jokes."

"Swear?"

"I swear." I held out my pinky. She locked hers with mine. We touched thumbs. The contract was sealed.

"You know Joe?" she asked, leaning forward again. I turned around, and she put the comb back in my hair.

"Joe who?"

"Malloy."

"Of course I know Joe Malloy. Malloy's grandson. You like him, Jazz?"

I could feel Jazz's face turn red without having to turn around. It was like it was putting out some kind of heat that I could feel on the back of my neck.

"Don't tell nobody, Ali," she said desperately. "But yeah. He kinda cute. And he nice. And he smart."

At this point I pretty much didn't want to talk about Jazz's eleven-year-old love life anymore. But I knew Joe Malloy, and the reality is, he was a pretty good choice. Never into no trouble. Always polite and respectful. No fighting, even though he could probably whoop anyone his age, and mine, on this block, because he grew up with Malloy training him to be a boxer, so at least I knew he could protect her. Joe was kind of geeky, too, which I liked. He was always dressed up. Shirt tucked in his pants. Pants up on his butt. Glasses. Braces. All of it. And he walked around like he was okay with that. Never caught him trying to fit in. Of all the too-cool knuckleheads running around this neighborhood, Jazz picked a good one, and I wanted to believe that was because she had a good example in me.

"Okay, Jazz, I won't tell."

"Not even Noodles?"

"Not even Noodles."

Finally Jazz was finishing up my braids. She had maybe two or three more to do. My scalp must've been numb, because I could no longer feel her tugging on the hair.

She stopped for a moment and reached down and grabbed my cup of tea. She had finished hers a half hour earlier, and she knew I wasn't going to finish mine, mainly because it got cold—I could never seem to finish it before it got cold. She liked it either way. "Can I ask you something, Ali?"

"Of course."

She slurped from the cup and made that ahh noise after she swallowed.

"You think Mom and Dad will ever get back together?"

I turned around and faced her again. Her face was pure innocence.

"Aw, Jazz, I don't know. I really don't. I know they still care about each other, though, and whether they get back together or not, I know they both love us."

Jazz grinned, big, and then took another sip of tea. I smiled back, the way a big brother does when he knows he's made his little sister feel better. Little girls shouldn't have to worry about their parents' issues, but I guess when you're eleven going on eighteen, it's normal.

Jazz finished braiding the last patch of hair I had left. Then, like we always do after she does my hair, we passed out on the couch. We were out until around five thirty, when my mother came clunking through the door. I opened my eyes just enough to see what was on the TV. News again. We had been asleep for almost three hours. I looked over at my mother, who was like a blur moving fast around the room. My eyes still had sleep in them, but once I blinked a few times, I could see her clearly getting ready for her next job. Changing bags.

Taking one pair of heels out, putting another pair of heels in. Same flats on her feet, for the train. Keys jingling. Fridge open, dinner in the Tupperware with the burgundy top tossed into the bag. She finally noticed I was awake. She gazed at me and Jazz for a moment, and smiled.

"Hi, baby," she said softly.

"Hi, Mom," I replied, half-asleep.

"I'm gone to work. Take care of Jazz. Love you."

"Love you too," I mumbled.

She bent down and kissed Jazz on the head. Then she left. Click, click. Door locked. Flats don't make the *click-clack* sound that heels do going down the steps, but I could still hear her. Door open. I could hear her speaking to someone but couldn't make it out. Door closed. Then stomping coming up the steps. I could tell the person coming was skipping every other step. Then bang bang bang on the door. *Bang, bang, bang* again. Jazz moaned and rolled over on the couch, burying her head in a cushion.

I got up and staggered over to the door.

"Who is it?" I asked, loud enough for the person outside to hear, but soft enough not to wake Jazz.

"Ali," the voice came back, loud.

"Shush, man, Jazz is asleep," I whispered while unlocking and cracking the door. It was Noodles.

"Oh, aight, my bad, man. Just wanna see what time we meeting up tonight," he said. His excitement was kind of an overload to me because I was barely awake.

"I don't know, man, nine?" I figured nine was a good time,

because that would put us at the party around nine thirty. And I figured hopefully, just because it's a MoMo party, it would be jumping by then.

"Cool, meet us on the stoop. Man, this is gonna be so live. So live. We gonna be in there, Ali!" Noodles started bouncing around like he had to pee.

"Yeah, we in there," I said lazily. I slid my hand through the crack in the door and gave Noodles a five before closing it. I heard him take about three steps and then jump down the rest of the stairs. The fool was so excited, I thought he was going to mess around and break a leg before we even got to the party. Then I thought, if that happens, Needles and I are still going. One monkey don't stop the show.

★ 8 ★

Around seven I jumped in the shower. The shower has always been a place for me to think about stuff and just, sort of, work my nerves out in my head. Sometimes I rap, but most times I just throw punches at nothing. I know—crazy, but I really do swing at the water, jabs, uppercuts, hooks, pretending that the splash is the sweat spraying off somebody. It sounds more violent than it actually is. I like to pretend sometimes that I have some kind of superpower or out-of-this-world fighting skills, but most of the time it's just me beating the crap out of my own nerves. And knowing I was leaving Jazz alone and going to a party I just had to go to, but had no business being at, I was nervous. And after thinking about even hitting on an older girl, a woman, the nerves really started to take over.

I started throwing punches in the shower way back when Jazz was a baby. When John was doing his three years and Doris took on the second job to keep us from begging, I was expected to step up and pick up the slack when it came to Jazz.

Well, not really, but I felt that way. Like I had to be a big boy all of a sudden because now I had a baby sister to look after. But I was only like six or seven, and the truth is, Doris would've never left me in charge that young. She had Ms. Brenda, from upstairs, come down and babysit us both every night, making sure Jazz was all changed and fed, and burped and put to sleep. But Ms. Brenda also could tell that I wanted to be a part of it all, so she would let me hold Jazz and try to feed her. But almost every time Ms. Brenda would put Jazz in my arms, Jazz would start crying and screaming and squirming all over the place. I remember always feeling really nervous, like I was doing something wrong. Like I wasn't holding her neck right. Like I wasn't going to feed her enough, or burp her the right way. Like I wasn't going to be a good big brother like my mom wanted.

It got so bad that I literally got scared to hold Jazz at all. My mother, working with mentally ill people every day, noticed I was acting funny and started asking me questions. She even had a friend, Mrs. Staley, who let us come to her house on Sundays to talk. Mrs. Staley would listen to everything I would say about how I was afraid to "break" Jazz, and she would ask me questions, which I always thought were stupid, and then give me advice that ended up being really good and helpful.

One day when I was visiting Mrs. Staley, she just flat-out said, "Allen, I been thinking. You know what you doing? Beating yourself up."

That was the first time I had ever heard anyone say I was

beating myself up, and I wasn't sure what it meant, so I didn't know what to say.

"Son, what that means is you just being too hard on yourself," my mother said. "Babies are babies. They cry because that's just what they do. Jazz cries when I hold her too, sometimes. It's okay."

"So what am I supposed to do?" I asked. I remember feeling like I was going to cry.

Mrs. Staley smiled. She had a gold tooth in the front that I always thought was funny. "Well, I been thinking about that too," she said, excited. "When you start beating yourself up, just fight back."

Of course, that sounded like the dumbest idea ever. I mean, it didn't make any sense—it was like one of those "smarty" answers that I wasn't sure was supposed to be serious or not. So I laughed. But then I could tell she was serious, so I asked how was I supposed to fight myself back. And that's when they came up with the punching-in-the-shower thing. They figured it would be a pretty easy thing for me to do since I had just started boxing training with Malloy, and all that stuff. Ever since then, whenever I get nervous or feel any kind of pressure, I two-piece the hell out of the shower water, pretending I'm in a real fight. Nothing wrong with pretending. It works.

I could smell something coming from the kitchen as I dried off. I cracked the door to let some of the shower steam out so the mirror would clear up, as I planned to examine every bump and hair on my face. The scent came right into the bathroom and wrapped around my nose like a winter scarf. So good.

"You smell that?" Jazz shouted from the kitchen.

I laughed because if there's one thing Jazz loved to brag about, it was her cooking. This is the only time she gave herself nicknames.

"Yeah, I smell it!" I yelled back. "What is it?"

"Chef Jammin' Jazzy's Spa-ghetto," she said in a French accent, which made it even funnier, since she had made an Italian meal.

"Spaghetto, huh?" I got as close to the mirror as possible and picked at the only pimple I had, which was right in the middle of my forehead. It was like trying to figure out how to cover up a bull's-eye.

"Yep, and you better come and get it while it's hot, because ain't nothing worse than cold Spaghetto!" Jazz clanged pots and dishes around in the kitchen.

I kept picking at the bump until the smell of Jazz's food got the best of me. I gave the nasty monster on my forehead one last look, and told myself that it would be dark in the party anyway. Plus, I'm wearing the Yankees hat, so screw it. Time to eat.

I threw on some basketball shorts and went to the kitchen, where Jazz was already piling up my plate. I stuck my face in the pot and took a big whiff.

"Back up, Ali, before you drop boogers in it!" Jazz said, slapping at me.

She finished plopping the sauce on my noodles and then pulled a few pieces of toast out of the oven.

"Garlic bread," she said. "Made the garlic butter myself, because I'm Chef Jammin' Jazzy."

I laughed. "Yeah, you jammin', you jammin'."

I took a seat on the couch. Jazz started making another big plate. Too big for her. I knew who it was for. Every time Jazz cooks, the same thing happens. We don't know how he always knows, but he always does.

Sure enough, as soon as she put a piece of garlic toast on that plate, there was a knock at the door. I got up, took the chain off the door, and turned the knob just enough to unclick it. Noodles came waltzing in like he lived with us. Jazz met him at the couch, gave him a hug as usual, and handed him his plate. No questions asked. No hellos or anything. Just a "Thanks, Jazz" and a forkful of food.

"I thought I said nine, Nood," I teased. I looked straight ahead at the TV as if I wasn't talking to him.

"Yeah, but you know I can smell Jazz's cooking through the wall," Noodles said, slurping and making the face that got him that nickname. "What is this anyway?"

"My world-famous Spaghetto. Duh," Jazz chimed in, perfectly on cue.

"And what's in it?" Noodles asked. It didn't really matter what was in it. He was going to eat it anyway. We all were.

"A whole bunch of love, fool," Jazz said. What that really meant was, a whole lot of everything was in it. Whatever she could get her hands on in the fridge. Leftover this and leftover that. It was like a spaghetti gumbo.

I looked at Noodles. He was eating like he hadn't had any food since the last time Jazz cooked, which was three days ago. He held his plate right up to his face and shoveled the noodles in like a prisoner afraid of it being snatched away. I looked over at Jazz, expecting her to have her usual devilish grin she always has whenever she thinks people like her food, but instead she looked concerned.

"Dang, Noodles, don't forget to breathe," Jazz said.

"Dang, Jazz, don't forget to shut up," Noodles snapped back in a silly voice.

Jazz laughed and shook her head.

"Anyway, it ain't because your food is so good, it's just because I'm starving. I mean, it's good, but . . . ," Noodles mumbled while shoving another forkful in his mouth.

Jazz smirked. She knew it was a combination of both. So did I. All I could think about was the first day Jazz and Noodles met, and Jazz asked him if his mom didn't cook. It was like déjà vu. Then the old soul in her kicked in. "You want me to fix a plate up for Needles?"

Noodles never even looked up. "Nope. He fine."

"But if you this hungry, he gotta be pretty hungry too, right?" Jazz persisted.

"I don't know," Noodles said, shoving a piece of garlic toast in his mouth. Crumbs exploded all over his lap.

"You don't know?" Jazz asked, now getting upset, the Doris in her coming out.

Noodles always had a soft spot for Jazz. No matter how much of a jerk he was to almost everyone else, Jazz had him wrapped around her finger. It was like she was the sibling he wished he had.

"Naw, I don't know, Jazz. He didn't seem hungry when I left," Noodles explained, a little nicer this time.

Jazz and I looked at each other. He didn't seem hungry? What was that supposed to mean? Jazz was pissed.

Noodles finished off what was left of his meal, set the plate on the floor, and wiped his mouth with the back of his wrist. I already knew that he wouldn't take Needles a plate. I also knew that eventually we would have to finish that conversation about why he treats Needles like he doesn't love him, when we all know he does.

"Y'all got some soda?" Noodles asked.

I was about to get up and grab him one, when Jazz shut me down.

"Nope, we don't," she said.

"Juice?" Noodles asked.

"Nope."

We had juice and soda. We always did. Noodles knew we did too. But I got what Jazz was up to—making it a point to not give Noodles anything else because of how he treated Needles. I was cool with that.

Jazz stood at the kitchen sink with one hand on her hip. She gave Noodles a look, reached over and turned on the sink faucet, and then did a Vanna White hand gesture as if saying, "Come and get your prize . . . New York City tap water."

Noodles looked at her, surprised. "Come on, Jazz.

Seriously?" He stood up, brushed the bread crumbs onto the floor, rolled his eyes, and walked toward the door.

"Nine, Ali," he said, almost like he was giving me some kind of order. Then he closed the door behind him, hard enough to be disrespectful but not hard enough for me to come and kick his tail. Or better yet, for Jazz to kick his tail.

I picked his plate up off the floor and tried to scoop up some of the bigger bread crumbs.

"What's happening at nine?" Jazz asked. She turned the faucet off.

"Nothing much," I said, walking the plate over to the sink. "Hey, can you make Needles a plate for me? Gonna take it to him later."

Jazz's eyes lit up, and her smile spread wide as she scrambled through Doris's mountain of Tupperware, searching for the perfect bowl.

★ **9** ★

I checked my cell phone. No missed calls. It was 8:51 p.m., nine minutes before meet-up time. I could hear Jazz talking on the phone in her bedroom, probably to one of her homegirls. I wondered for a second if it could've been Joe Malloy. But I'm sure it wasn't, just because Jazz never went a night without gossiping and giggling with one of her friends. I could tell by her voice that she was already lying down, and had the phone lying on the side of her face. That was her routine every night. She'd be asleep soon. Sometimes she fell asleep with the phone still on!

I laced up my new sneakers, then unlaced and laced them better. Pulled the tongue of the shoe up. Scrubbed the toe with a spitty finger. Gotta be perfect. You never know who might be at this party. Might be the finest woman I ever seen, and she might be looking for a smooth brother like me, with clean shoes.

I checked my pockets and made sure I had everything. Keys, phone, a few bucks. I went in the fridge and grabbed the "Spaghetto" for Needles. Then I peeked in Jazz's room only enough for me to see in, but not for her to see out. I knew that if she saw all the new clothes, she would start asking questions, and wouldn't stop asking them until she got the truth. Two things are for sure, Jazz ain't no dummy, and she is unbelievably persistent. She'd be a great lawyer, but knowing her, she'll end up a chef, or an Oprah.

"Sleep?" I asked calmly, like nothing was up.

"Hold on," she said to whoever was on the other end. "Naw, not yet."

"Oh, okay," I said. I couldn't really see much, but the light from the hallway created a shadow stripe across her face. Just like I thought, the phone was lying on her cheek. "I'm gonna run this food next door to Needles. Probably hang for a little bit."

Jazz propped her head up. It was like she knew I was lying but didn't want to say anything. She knew something was up—she knew something was happening at nine.

"Okay, Ali," she said with a smirk. "I'll probably be asleep. I'll see you tomorrow morning." Jazz was such a grown-up.

"Just call me if you need me. I'll be next door," I said lightly, but I suddenly felt the opposite—like my heart was heavy, sinking into my stomach. Like I was making a mistake. Like this was a bad idea. But that bad feeling lifted as soon as I closed Jazz's door and took a glance down at the kicks I had on. Perfect. I mean, not a mark on them and not a lace twisted. Them bad boys were clean enough for a cop to harass me just for having them on. I had three black boys in a Benz with tinted windows, all on my feet.

I texted my mom. GOING NEXT DOOR. BACK B4 CURFEW. Then I grabbed my hat and ran upstairs to knock on Ms. Brenda's door. She answered with her usual "We all family" face on, which is why everyone loved her. She never needs to watch both of us anymore, but sometimes she comes down to watch Jazz if I'm hanging out. Doris was okay with this mainly because she was always working late, and I would never get to hang out if I had to wait for her to come home first. She was cool like that sometimes. Plus she knew where I was, which was usually either over at Noodles and Needles's, or having a late training session at Malloy's. As long as I was in the house before midnight, my mother had no problems, and tonight I planned on being back by eleven. I mean, I really was going next door. We were just going to go somewhere else after that. So it was only a half lie.

Ms. Brenda looked like she was made of cookie dough. Her cheeks were puffy, and her lips were big and her chest was even bigger. Sometimes, on hot days, when she wore low-cut shirts, you could see the baby powder she put down there to stay cool, most of which was lost somewhere deep in her cleavage. Everything about her was soft. Her hair, her voice, everything. Especially her heart, when it came to us.

"Now, let me guess what you want, Allen," she said, one hand on her chin, pretending like she was thinking. "You want me to come down there and mind the place until Doris gets home, because you want to run around all times of the night."

I smiled. I was a little embarrassed because she thought I

was just joking, but this time I was really going to be breaking the rules.

"Just for an hour, then my mom'll be home."

"Where you goin', next door?"

"Yes, ma'am," I said nervously.

"Does your mama know?" she asked.

"Yes, ma'am, of course." It almost hurt to say it.

Ms. Brenda looked at me skeptically, then nodded her head. "Okay, Allen. Lord knows we gotta look out for one another. Ain't nobody else gonna do it if we don't." She grabbed her keys from the corner table by the door, and a book that looked like one of those romance novels they sell in the supermarket. She also grabbed her cell phone and her cordless house phone, and gathered up the bottom of her long nightgown, which looked like nothing more than a big frilly silk sack with a hole cut for her head to go through.

"What y'all boys up to anyway?" she asked, her voice comforting like a cup of hot chocolate.

I didn't answer, just smiled awkwardly and headed down the steps in front of her. Ms. Brenda moved a lot slower than me. Or maybe I was just moving really fast because I had to get outside to meet the guys.

Once we got to my door, I unlocked it. Then my phone started buzzing. It was a text from my mom.

OK. BRENDA THERE?

"It's open, Ms. Brenda. I really appreciate this!" I said while trying not to run down the last flight of stairs. When I got to the front door, I double-checked my shoes. Still fresh.

Then I put my Yankees hat on, pulled it down low by the brim, and twisted it a little to the left. Sharp. Then I texted my mom back. YES.

As soon as the thick night air hit me, Noodles called out, "Yooooo!"

He was standing at the bottom of his stoop holding a piece of paper.

"Yoooooo!" I stepped lightly down the stoop. "Where's Needles?"

"He coming." Noodles handed me the paper. "Check this out."

It was a sketch. One of the best I had ever seen him do. It wasn't a superhero, though. It was a girl. A slammin' girl!

"Is this Tasha?"

"Yeah, what you think?" Noodles asked. "I did it straight from memory. Think I'm gonna give it to her tonight."

He drew her face almost dead-on. It was pretty impressive. "Man, with skills like this, you might actually have a shot!"

We laughed, and as Noodles started folding the drawing up, the door of their building swung open. Somebody should've been playing some theme music. Some Jay-Z or one of them smooth seventies songs, because Needles looked like he needed some to go along with his outfit. I mean, everything fit him perfectly. The shirt, the pants, the shoes. Everything. Noodles looked pretty fresh too, but I could tell by the way he was walking that his shoes were too small. Still looked fly, though, but not as fly as Needles.

"Yoooo, Ali," Needles said as he skipped down the steps

like he was walking on air. I could tell he felt good just by the way he spoke to me. It caught me off guard. Confidence was all over him. He had his yarn and his needles with him too, of course, but even that couldn't distract from his clothes. My man looked like a stack of money.

I gave Needles the container of Spaghetto.

"From Jazz. Pretty good, too."

"Tell her thanks," he said.

"Of course—"

"Man, forget about all that," Noodles interrupted. "What I wanna know is, are we good? We in there?"

"You already know. We in there," I said, feeling a rush all over me.

We headed down the block toward Tasha and MoMo's house. Needles had his yarn and needles tucked under his arm while he forked through the spaghetti noodles, slurping the red sauce. He kept trying to freestyle about how dope the party was going to be, but kept interrupting himself by shoveling food into his mouth. I prayed he wouldn't have an outburst and spray tomato sauce all over us, but I was happy he got to eat something. And that he was so pumped.

Tasha and MoMo lived just a block down, but it seemed like a whole other borough just because the blocks were so much different. On one side of Decatur and Lewis, where we live, there's, well, where we live. A bunch of people like us. Good folks, with a little edge to them, as my mother puts it. Some trash on the sidewalk, or sometimes a pissy mattress or a stained-up couch. Brown-bag beer bottles in the hands of old men and tatted-up teenagers. Babies crying, an occasional fight, but also a lot of laughing. As a matter of fact, just a lot of noise in general.

But on the other side of Decatur and Lewis, peace and quiet. Trees and flowers line the block. Every brownstone has a light post outside, so it's always well lit at night. No trash. It was the "Cosby" side of the street. I figured it must've been the part of the neighborhood where Doris was always talking about all the white people were moving into. Gotta be.

We walked down the block toward Lewis Ave, none of us saying a word. I felt like we were just soaking it all up, and if Noodles and Needles felt anything like me, then the walk seemed more like we were gliding down the street. I just wished that it wasn't so dark and that there were more people outside to see us this fly. I couldn't wear the same outfit tomorrow. Shoot, I knew I couldn't wear that outfit ever again because I couldn't have Doris and Jazz asking me where I got it from. Doris would kill John, and Jazz would . . . well, Jazz would kill John too, just because he ain't give her no fancy clothes. So I was just enjoying the moment. We all were.

"You know where they live, right, Nood?" I asked as we crossed over Lewis Ave.

"Yeah, I know. Middle of the block. Right side," he said. Then he breathed in, deep. "Is it just me or is the air fresher on this side of Lewis?"

We all busted out laughing. We all knew Noodles was joking, but, you know, it did seem like the air was different.

After another minute or so, Noodles stopped walking.

"We here."

I looked around, confused. I couldn't hear anything, or see anything that looked anything like a party.

"Where?"

"Here." Noodles pointed to the house. "This is it. Middle of the block. Right side."

The house looked like every other house on the block. Nine windows, three floors, big wooden door, black iron gate. A typical Brooklyn brownstone.

"Man, ain't nobody out here. I don't even hear no music," I said. He didn't know what he was talking about.

"Man, you think I don't know where Tasha live? I love that girl!" he said. "I know where my future wife stay at, man!"

Well, that was a good point, and it wouldn't surprise me if Noodles grew up and started stalking Tasha. He was just that kind of dude, plus he really, really liked her. He wouldn't have had to trip so hard if she just told him the truth, that she liked him too.

"This is it," he repeated. But still we stood in front of the house for a minute, hoping to get some kind of sign. I just couldn't understand why we couldn't hear no music. On our block, whenever anybody had a party, you could hear the music so loud that it sounded like the DJ was in the bed with you. The bass made the walls vibrate. But here, at MoMo's house, one of the most popular parties in Brooklyn, silence.

A gypsy cab came cruising down the street suspiciously. Once it got close to where we were standing, it stopped. The back door opened, and out came a woman, all legs.

She walked past us, her hips swinging like nothing we

had ever seen before, like she had an invisible hula hoop around her waist. She walked right through the gate of the house Noodles said was Tasha and MoMo's. We watched her as she tapped on the door lightly. Three times. Tap, tap, tap. The door opened, and the music came bursting out like gunfire. And as soon as the door closed, it was gone. I almost fell over in shock! What the? The house was soundproofed?

"Told y'all," Noodles said, shooting me a look.

"You were right, and so was she," I said, biting my bottom lip. She was out of my league, but hey, it can't hurt to fantasize. I looked down at my shoes. Made it all the way down there with no scuffs. Still perfect. We all did a once-over of our clothes, making sure everything was okay and that we looked older than we really were. No sauce on Needles, thank God. I pulled my hat down, and Noodles brushed his hair with the palm of his hand. Needles blew into his palm and sniffed, then pulled a pack of gum out of his pocket and popped a piece in his mouth. Then he blew into his palm again.

Me and Noodles stood there staring at him. He was more prepared than we were! I didn't have gum, and I know Noodles didn't either.

Needles caught us staring. "What?"

"Nothing."

"You ready, Bruce Wayne?" Noodles teased.

I pulled out my phone and texted my father. I almost forgot. HERE.

Then the password, which I realized Tasha never told us, but we peeped anyway—three taps. Tap, tap, tap.

The door opened, and there was Tasha. She was looking amazing like always, but Noodles was looking at her like he didn't just see that girl with all them legs come in right before we did. The older girl. That boy was stuck on Tasha.

Tasha manned the entranceway, which led to the open area where all the people were. This was where she checked IDs, took money, and all that kind of stuff. I didn't see no security or bouncers or anything like that, but I guess if anyone tried anything crazy with Tasha, the little sister of MoMo, every person in this place would take turns handing out whoopings to him. It would be the worst day of that fool's life.

Tasha looked stunned to see us, and I knew why. She didn't think we would come. Not after she said we had to bring Needles. She didn't even give us the password, but we still showed up.

"Well, well, well," Tasha started in her typical butthead way. "I can't believe y'all actually came!" The music was so loud, she was practically screaming so we could hear her.

"Yep!" I shouted. "And look who we brought with us!" I stepped to the side so she could see Needles, all dressed up, so she knew we kept our part of the deal and called her bluff.

Tasha's eyes bugged. "Whoa! Look at you, Needles! Looking like a million bucks!" She gave him a big hug. He stood stiff, uncomfortable. He said something back to Tasha, but we couldn't hear him. He was still holding the Spaghetto container, which had nothing left in it but streaks of red sauce and a plastic fork.

"What about me!" Noodles shouted, all jealous.

Tasha looked at him. Up. Then down. Then up again. She smiled and got real close to his ear to tell him something. I don't know what she said but it made him smile wide enough to split his face in two.

"Listen, y'all, please, please, please lay low. And stay far away from MoMo—he knows y'all, and he knows y'all don't belong in here. Don't blow this or he's gonna kill me. Got it?" Tasha was nervous.

"Got it!"

"Got it!"

"Yep."

"Okay, cool," Tasha said, nodding hard. Then she began shaking her head. "I don't even know why I'm letting y'all in here," she grumbled.

"Oh, quick question, Tash," I said, because I had to know. "Why can't you hear the music outside?"

Tasha laughed. "Because MoMo had the whole basement soundproofed so that our parents won't know nothing about this kind of stuff! They not here anyway, but you know, no complaints from the neighbors! This ain't y'all block! Our neighbors don't play around here! It's quiet, and they like it that way!" she said, shouting to be heard over the heavy bass.

I knew it! I was instantly impressed. I thought MoMo was the man before, but now I was realizing that he was a party genius.

"Aight, y'all, go ahead in," Tasha hollered. She grabbed the container from Needles and set it to the side. Then she ushered us into a basement heaven.

★ 10 ★

A MoMo party. I was at a freakin' MoMo party. At fifteen. What more could anyone ask for? The party was set up pretty simple. A big open space where people were dancing and grinding on each other; a couch, where people were sitting and making out; a hallway—I assumed the bathroom was down there; a DJ in one corner; and a table with drinks along the back wall. Christmas lights lined the ceiling—the only lights in the whole place. I thought that was pretty cool. I could smell smoke, but it wasn't too strong, and I recognized a few faces from the neighborhood—faces of some friendly folks, and faces of some not-so-friendly folks. As a matter of fact, there were some downright gully, straight-out-the-pen dudes in there, with face scars to go with their gold chains, but I tried not to stare or nothing. Just played it cool. It was the top of the top and the lowest of the lows all in one room, shaking it up.

The women—wow—they were all gorgeous, though. It's like MoMo had some sort of requirement as to what kind of ladies he let in his parties. They were all beautiful, like models, and they were barely dressed. I mean, revealing. Not a bad thing but nothing I was used to. Not on this level. This ain't no fifteen-year-old party. These girls ain't look like they had to text their daddies to tell them they made it there safe.

I bobbed my head to the music and scoped the room. Keep it cool, I thought to myself. I figured Needles and Noodles were still right with me, but when I turned around, neither of them was. Damn. I looked around. Noodles was back by the front door talking to Tasha. He was showing her the picture he drew for her, and looked like he was really putting in work. For once she seemed to be biting, or at least she didn't look like she was throwing him a bunch of shade, like she usually did. Maybe with no one around, Tasha softened up. I smiled at the fact that with all these girls in here, all these older girls, he still goes for Tasha. What a softy. But I wasn't surprised.

Who I was surprised by, though, was Needles. He was already in the middle of the dance floor, moving like a madman. He still had his yarn and needles in his hand, and was waving them back and forth. I had never seen him dance, and I never would've guessed that he could move the way he was moving, only because he was always so laidback. Maybe music was just his thing. He could rap, and apparently he could dance, too. And by dance, I mean dude was a dancing machine! The crowd started to notice him, started cheering him on. It made me a little nervous, only because I didn't want anyone from the hood to recognize him. They would fly us out of there so fast, we wouldn't know what hit us. But I couldn't help but watch. I mean, he was good. I wanted to grab Noodles so he could see, but I knew he wouldn't want to leave Tasha, so I didn't bother. It was probably better he didn't see anyway, actually. Knowing Noodles, he probably would've freaked out and ran and snatched Needles up, not even realizing how dope it all was.

A circle formed around Needles as he dropped to the floor and brought it back up again. He did a few spins, and popped and locked his body like he was raised in the eighties. He moved and slid around like he ain't have no bones, with a cool grin on his face the whole time. It was as if this was the first time he had ever heard music, and he just couldn't control himself. A few girls jumped in the circle and started bumping their butts up against him. They laughed, and I could tell that they were giving him some rhythm, but Needles was so caught up in dancing, he wasn't even paying the girls no attention.

"Give it to her!" I yelled, being careful not to say his name out loud. I hoped he would get the message and dance with the girls. I just laughed and laughed, he looked so happy. Then one of the girls came in front of him and faced him. She waved her body and bumped against his. Then she wrapped her arms around his waist and pulled him close to her, as close as anyone could get. Close enough for jean zippers to lock on each other.

"Owwwwwwww!" someone else yelled as everybody egged him on.

Needles suddenly stiffened. It was like his muscles tensed up, as if he had even more bones in his body than he started with. It was like something clicked, and he froze up. He waved the girl off and stepped away. Thankfully, everybody just jumped in the circle, giving Needles the chance to disappear in the crowd.

"Yo! Yo!" I screamed out and waved so he could see me. He made his way back over, all out of breath.

"That was crazy, man!" I said.

"Thanks, man," he said, huffing. He slapped me five, then wiped the sweat from his forehead.

"I didn't know you could dance like that! You could be on TV!" I couldn't get a hold of myself—I was just so shocked at Needles doing all those moves. Every girl in the room wanted him. He got the party started. He was the man. Syndrome, what? I wished Noodles had seen.

Needles and I pushed through the crowd to the drink table. I started reaching for a beer at first, but when Needles reached for a soda, I reached for a soda too. Sidenote: There was no bartender, and I didn't see no strippers, neither. I mean, pretty girls, yeah, but not strippers. Matt, my sparring buddy, didn't know what he was talking about.

We had been at the party for about thirty minutes when I spotted the girl with the legs. The one I saw when we were coming in. I checked my shoes. Still clean. I took a sip of my soda and decided it was time to make a move.

"I'm gonna go talk to that girl, man. You gonna be okay?" I asked Needles. I knew he'd be fine, but I still had to ask.

He nodded—"I'm straight, man"—and made his way to a corner on the other side of the room. He leaned against the wall and began to fool with his yarn. It was dark, so nobody could really see him, which was a good thing. It's weird to see a dude with a bunch of fly clothes on standing in a corner of a crazy party, knitting. Most folks just wouldn't understand.

I glanced over at the front door. Noodles was still over there with Tasha. Perfect. Wanted to keep a close eye on my boys. I put on my cool, which wasn't much, but on this night, way more than normal, and strutted over to where the girl with the legs was standing. She was sipping something pink. I think it was the punch they had on the table. I heard someone call it "loose juice," so I guessed it was spiked. In my mind I ran through a couple of icebreakers. "Dope party, right?" or "You look absolutely beautiful tonight" or "Didn't I see you coming in?" None of them were sticking, so I figured I would do what Doris always tells me to do when her friends come over—just open my mouth and say hello.

"Hey," I said. She didn't hear me over the music, thankfully, because once "Hey" came out, I realized how lame "Hey" was.

So I tried again.

"How are you?" I asked, a little louder. I knew she heard me because she smiled.

"Fine!" She was yelling, but I could still tell she had a nice voice.

I took a sip of my soda. "You look amazing tonight," I said. Then I suddenly felt the need to explain myself. "And

I don't mean that in a sleazy way. I just mean you really look nice."

I lied. I meant it in the usual way, which was sleazy, but I figured that half the men in the party had already tried their hands, probably all saying that she looks amazing. "You look amazing" was probably getting pretty boring to her.

She smiled again and took another sip of the loose juice.

"Thanks," she said. Then she held out her hand in that soft girly way. If we wasn't at a MoMo party and I was sixty years old, I would've kissed it.

"I'm Candace."

"Ali. Nice to meet you, Candace."

Candace shifted her weight from one leg to the other. I took another swig of my soda and tried not to stare at her legs. She smelled fantastic, and I could tell she did that thing Doris does with perfume. A dab on the wrists, a dab on the elbows, and a dab behind the ears.

It got awkward for a moment. I didn't know what to say next. But once she finished her drink, I just offered to go and get her another. It was the only thing I could think of. My only opening. It was just like in the movies. I went over to the drink table. When I got there, MoMo was standing in front of it, all hugged up with some girl who was clearly drunk or high or something. I pulled my hat further down over my face and scooped the punch as fast as I could without making a mess all over the place.

Once I made it back over to Candace, without spilling a drop, which was important to me, her head was being talked off by some other joker with a fat gold chain on, and big diamond earrings in his ear that I could tell were fake. The reason I knew they were fake is because I looked at his shoes. Busted. Ain't no man with busted shoes can afford no real dime-size diamond earrings. My shoes were spotless, and I couldn't afford them either, but I was only fifteen. Just saying. She was sipping at another cup of punch that I guess "Busted Shoe Dude" had brought to her. I didn't want to make a fuss about it, so I just walked away and went looking for another girl to talk to. Meanwhile, since I'd poured the cup of punch, I decided to have a sip myself. Why not? It tasted just like soda, but I felt a little cooler drinking it.

I knew it was time to check on my boys again. Needles was still in the corner, knitting. The party that he got started was now happening, full-out, but now he was all of a sudden too shy to participate. Noodles was dancing with Tasha in the front area. They weren't too close to each other, but still, MoMo would've flipped if he caught them.

Right when I took the last sip of loose juice, I felt a tap on my shoulder.

"Where did you go?" Candace's voice and sweet breath came down on me like summer heat.

"Oh," I said, my mind going blank. She was looking for me! "I went to get you a drink, but when I came back over, you were being entertained," I said. I was pretty proud of myself for saying, "You were being entertained." That was smooth.

"Yeah, by a clown," she said, laughing.

I smiled. "Yeah, it looked that way."

Candace downed what had to be half a cup of loose juice. She twisted her face up as if it tasted nasty, but it didn't.

"You gonna dance with me, or what?" she said, demanding. She put my hands on her hips and started swaying them right to left and back again. I couldn't believe it. And I couldn't believe where my hands were. She kept rocking back and forth, and my hands kept following her, back and forth, to the beat of the music. I couldn't have moved them if I tried.

We started grooving. I won't pretend like I'm some kind of spectacular dancer, but for some reason I was feeling it. I mean, I was really moving, and everything was on rhythm, which is usually pretty tough for me unless I got on boxing gloves, and even then it ain't so easy. It might have been the loose juice. I wasn't drunk or nothing, but I was definitely a lot looser than normal. Candace smiled and gave me all kinds of sexy looks as she danced around me and beside me and behind me. She was everywhere, and all over me, and man, I was loving it, but I acted like it was nothing. I pretended like I was used to older hot girls showing me love. At one point she was in front of me grinding. I moved my hands up around her waist and rested my chin on her neck like a professional. I mean, I've grinded before at other parties, but never with no grown woman at a MoMo party.

I could not believe this was happening. I didn't even have to sneak a feel. She took my hands and put them on her thighs and everywhere, and the whole time I'm trying to keep cool and not be fifteen. I kissed her on her neck. Just a nibble.

I don't know where it came from, but it seemed like the right thing to do. She didn't say nothing, so I kept doing it. My brain was going crazy. All I kept thinking was, This is unbelievable. I tried to back up a few times—I didn't want her to feel me or anything, because that would be embarrassing. But every time I pulled away, she yanked me closer.

I don't know how long we were dancing. It might have been an hour, but it could have been twenty minutes. Both of us were soaked, and Candace had taken off her shirt and just had on a tank top. Her hair started to frizz up. She grabbed my hand and started leading me through the crowd. I had no idea where she was taking me. There was a hallway right by where the DJ was set up. She led me down it. It was dark, but Christmas lights lined the ceiling there, too, so I could see people. Some were making out against the wall. Some were talking. Some were flicking lighters, but I wasn't sure what they were lighting, and didn't want to look long enough to find out.

Halfway down the hallway was a room. Okay, so Matt was right about the room. Candace took me in there, and I realized then that things were getting way more serious than I had expected. She didn't close the door. She just threw herself on me, wrapping her arms around my neck and kissing me. And while my brain was still going, "I can't believe it," another part of me was starting to get nervous. I mean, I had made out with girls, but something told me we were going to be doing more than kissing and touching and stuff. I wasn't really ready to go all the way. I had never done it before. But

I also didn't want to come across as a stupid kid, so I just went with it and prayed something would happen to distract her. Sort of like how John busted in on Noodles and me when we were about to fight in the kitchen. I needed another one of those random interruptions. A drunk guy, a sick girl. Anything. If not, I was going to have to go all the way. My mother always said that once you start a lie, you gotta keep lying. So if Candace and I were going to go all the way, I was going to have to either pretend like this was no big deal for me, or lie my way out of it. I mean, really, I don't even know how I'm thinking about all this—about anything—with this hot girl all over me.

It seemed like Candace was kissing me forever. I laid back on the bed, and she got right on top of me. She kissed me hard and then looked at me for a second and asked if I was all right.

"Yeah, I'm fine," I whispered, holding her tighter around the waist. For a second I thought she could tell I was nervous, but I tried to play it off by pulling her back down on top of me to kiss more. I wondered if she knew I was younger, and if she did, how come she didn't care? Maybe she was underage too. Maybe it was too dark for her to really see me. Maybe it was the liquor. She whispered something in my ear, but I couldn't make it out because it was kinda slurred. I think she said I kiss good. Something like that. Then she leaned up again and tried to undo my belt, and I know I should've been crazy amped, and let me tell you, part of me was, but another part of me was thinking that this girl didn't even really know me. She didn't even know my last name. And I just couldn't shake that thought. I knew that I would probably kick myself later, but I just didn't want to do it. I mean, I did. It's hard to explain. This girl on any other night, maybe would've been my first. But it wasn't the right time. I think I just couldn't get over the fact that it was all happening so fast, and it all was so awesome, but I was too uncomfortable.

Another crazy thought running through my head was whether or not I was going to lie to Noodles about it, or if I was going to tell him I was scared to go all the way. Probably lie. He's the type who would tease me about it until I was sixty, and then lie about how he had already done it before.

I had to figure out how to stop her. There was only one way I knew. As she pulled at my belt, I grabbed her hands and whispered, "Ah. I want to. But I don't have a rubber." I pretended to be bummed. Truth is, I don't really know how I felt. Maybe I really was, maybe I wasn't.

"It's all right," Candace whispered. "MoMo keeps them in here." What?!? She leaned over and slid her hand in the drawer of a night table beside the bed that I hadn't even noticed was there. When she pulled her hand out, she was holding a condom.

"Look what I found," she chirped, and at that moment I knew I was a goner. This is the story I was going to have to tell about my first time. A MoMo party, with a gorgeous drunk older girl, that for some reason I wasn't really comfortable with. Maybe Doris's training had made me soft, I thought. Naw, not soft, just safe.

Candace stared right at me while pulling her tank top

over her head. I wondered if she could see how nervous I was, if it was in my eyes. I wondered what my face looked like as I tried to play cool, like I had done this before. I wondered if I would have to unsnap her bra, something I definitely would not be good at. She reached for my belt again, and as soon as she got it undone, someone came running down the hall screaming.

"They fighting! They fighting!" the voice yelled. The music was loud, but those words cut through the throbbing bass.

I don't know what it is about the hood that when a person yells "They fighting!" everybody stops what they're doing and runs toward the fight. Logic says to run away from the fight, but there's nothing more entertaining than a good brawl.

Candace jumped off me and reached for her shirt. I didn't wait for her to put it back on because to me, this was more than just a fight, it was my excuse to bail. So I ran out of the room and into the hallway, where people were crowded and yelling. I jumped to try to see over the crowd. I couldn't. I could hear the skin-on-skin contact, though. The punches sounded clean, and painful. I pushed through the crowd to get closer to the action, at the same time trying to spot Needles and Noodles to make sure they were okay. It didn't seem like anyone was trying to stop the fight, so I guess there were no bouncers or security guards like I expected. If they weren't careful, this thing could turn into a free-for-all, I thought. I didn't want Needles to have to be involved in nothing like that, and I didn't want to be involved either. Once I got close enough to see, I couldn't tell who was getting pounded on, but whoever it was would thank God for life if they made it to the morning. I looked for Needles and Noodles. I glanced over to the corner where I'd seen Needles last. Not there. Maybe he had gone outside. Looked to the front. Didn't see Noodles, either. Tasha was standing just enough inside the party room to see what was going on. Her hand covered her mouth, and her face was wet with tears. Then I looked to another corner. There stood Noodles—looked like he had seen a ghost. I made my way over to him to see if he knew where Needles was.

"Yo! Where's Needles?" I put my hand on his shoulder.

He didn't respond. He just stood there, like he was going through some kind of shock or something. Like his head was empty.

"Nood!" I yelled. "Nood!" I stepped directly in front of his face. "Where's Needles?"

Noodles looked at me, and his face crumbled. All of a sudden, my legs felt funny. I felt like I was going to pass out. That look on his face told me that Needles was the person getting pounded on in the middle of that brawl. And his punk-ass brother was just standing there like a freakin' sissy, scared, watching it all unfold.

If I could've burned a hole in his face with my eyes, I would have. But there wasn't time to try. I turned toward the fight and thrust my way through the crowd. I normally would've been terrified, but I didn't have time to be scared. I had to get to Needles.

Once I entered the danger zone, all I could do was imagine myself training with Malloy. I'd never even had a real boxing match. And the way I always got my ass handed to me in spars was enough for me to know I wasn't the best. But I couldn't let them kill Needles, so I had to hope the training worked better outside the ring than inside. Fists tight, thumbs down. The guys beating on Needles didn't see me coming up from behind. I grabbed one by the shoulder and spun him around. Once he faced me, I gave him a stiff jab right to the nose. Didn't put too much arm into it. Snapped it just like Malloy said, and put him right to sleep.

One thing Malloy always joked about was how guys who fight in the hood only know one punch, and that's a hook. They throw it wild and free, and because everybody does it, everybody gets caught with it. It's silly, but it's the way it is. Once I knocked the first guy out, the second guy turned around and noticed me. He did exactly what I expected him to do. A right hook. Before his fist was halfway to reaching me, I had already zapped him—boom boom boom—three times in the face. The hook never landed. Another one down.

I tried to scan the room as quickly as possible. I could see there was somebody else about to come at me, but another guy held him back. I couldn't recognize who he was. Maybe someone who recognized me from the neighborhood? No time to think. Somebody else came out of nowhere and snuffed me across the face. It stung, but surprisingly, my recovery time is pretty good, especially for such a lightweight. I stumbled but didn't fall. Somebody tried to hold him back as well, but he broke away and threw a few haymakers at me, missing. I could tell people were trying to break it up, but no one knew how.

He kept coming, but I switched to southpaw, which I could tell confused him. Malloy always said it would. Dude threw a jab but was way off. I gave a clean hook. I felt my hand meet his jawbone, and I knew that one of my knuckles was broken right then and there. It was my own damn fault—my fist wasn't closed tight enough and I knew it. Dude threw another jab, and I hit him with the same punch, followed by an uppercut. That might have been the first combination I had ever landed in real life. The pain shot up my arm, making my elbow and shoulder tingle, but I put it right on his chin, and through all the noise, I could still hear his teeth click. Out.

One guy left, which I was glad about because I was getting tired. He was a big guy. Much bigger than the other three. When people saw him coming, everybody just stepped out of the way. Nobody tried to stop him. He just football-tackled me. There was nothing I could do at that point but try to block my face. My lip busted right open when he landed on me. He caught me a few times right above the eye. I could feel a few random feet kicking me in my side, sideline suckers trying to get free licks. It felt like a house was on top of me; I could barely breathe. But I kept trying to punch him in the back and give everything I had to his ribs. A rib shot hurts like nothing else. I gave him what seemed like ten blows to the breadbasket, but they didn't faze him! I was outweighed big-time and was scared that if he didn't get off me, I would suffocate. Finally, out of nowhere, I heard Tasha's voice yell out, "Cops! Cops!"

The cops must've been called from the inside, because

the whole place was soundproof. Somebody could've started shooting in there and no one would hear it outside, which now, when I think about it, is pretty scary. The lights flicked on and everybody panicked, running like roaches. Big guy jumped off me and started scrambling, and I ran after him and hit him straight across the teeth. I pulled the punch from a special place, a place I didn't even know I had in me. I really wanted him to remember me every time he saw his gappy smile. It brought him to one knee, and I was good with that. I ran over to Needles and almost backed away again—he was lying there in a spreading puddle of his own blood. Oh my God. Oh my God. He was hurt bad. He wasn't moving. Oh my God. I fell to my knees.

"Come on, man! We gotta go!" I yelled to him. "Come on!" He rolled his head from one side to the other, and all I could think was, at least he's not dead. At least that.

Somehow I got Needles up and threw his arm around my shoulder.

"Nood, come on!" I shouted. He looked like he was drifting somewhere, having some sort of out-of-body experience. "Noodles!" I shrieked.

This snapped him out of it. He ran to his brother's side and swung Needles's free arm over his own, and together we propped Needles up, practically running him back across Lewis Ave, where we felt safe.

"You're gonna be okay, man. You're gonna be okay," I repeated over and over again. Needles kept trying to talk, but he couldn't get the words out. He kept spitting blood and grunting in pain. I kept looking to make sure his eyes were open—make sure he stayed conscious. He was barely moving his legs. We were practically dragging him.

Once we got to their house, we had a helluva time getting him up the steps. He could hardly move any part of his body. First we tried to drag him. He moaned in pain. No good. Then we tried carrying him, Noodles gripping under his arms, and me at his feet. Too awkward, and I was afraid Noodles would let go and Needles would bust his head on the steps. So I ended up just carrying him over my shoulder, like men always carry their wives in the old-time movies when they first get married. Needles was heavier than he looked, and I could feel his blood seep through my shirt as I took the steps, one by one. And judging from the smell coming from him, he had also pissed his pants.

After what seemed like forever, we got into their apartment. We took Needles straight to his room and laid him down.

"Help me get his clothes off," I ordered Noodles, who was just standing there looking at his broken-up brother with teary eyes. "Everything we do is gonna hurt him, so try to take it easy."

I leaned over Needles and slid his blood-soaked shirt up, wiggling it up his back slowly, and gently pulling it over his head.

"You get his pants, Nood."

Noodles looked at me like I asked him to kiss Needles on the mouth.

My hands started sweating. My mouth got dry. I was going to explode.

"Noodles! Take off his damn pants!" I barked.

Noodles jumped, now afraid of me, and started gingerly unbuckling Needles's belt. He looked so uncomfortable, as if this weren't his brother, his family, that I nudged him to one side and helped him shimmy Needles's jeans down. The blood made them look tie-dyed.

Needles twitched and grunted, as if his clothes had become full of tiny, invisible knives, shanking him with every tug of a pant leg. Expensive clothes should protect you from pain. They should be bulletproof, and bully proof, I thought, looking at all the gear John gave us, now a pile of damaged goods.

I told Noodles to get a wet towel so we could wipe the blood off Needles and I could see where the damage was.

"And y'all got some alcohol?" I asked as he started to run out of the room.

"Alcohol, like liquor?" Noodles responded.

"Naw, man. Alcohol like, the kind you clean stuff with. The kind you put on a cut."

Why the hell would I be asking for liquor?

"I don't know, let me look."

Somehow I knew they didn't have it, but while Noodles went to look for it, I spoke as encouragingly as I could to Needles.

"You gonna be good, man. We'll take care of you," I said, my voice starting to crack and slip into a cry. Needles opened his eyes for a moment, and then the lids fluttered closed again. "I'm so sorry. I swear. This shouldn't have happened. I shouldn't have left you alone." I felt so damned guilty. I was so ashamed. I felt like I had let my own brother down. I should've stayed close. I should've protected him. Instead I was off kissing some random girl.

Needles lifted his head just a little, maybe a half of a half of an inch off the pillow. His body jerked every few minutes, the syndrome, which seemed to be sending him into even more pain. Then I realized he was trying to tell me something. Tears were coming from his eyes. His head fell back down to the pillow, exhausted.

"It's okay, man. Just rest."

"Yo, he aight, Ali?" Noodles came running with a dripping towel. He stood by the door, too afraid to come any closer.

"Yeah. Get the alcohol?"

"Naw, man," Noodles said, defeated. "Not that kind."

I thought for a second as I looked over Needles's body, now starting to blue and purple up, the bruises looked like they were made with bats, not fists. Like tattoos of inkblots all over him. The cuts were mostly flesh wounds, but they still needed to be cleaned, or they would get infected and then who knows what could happen. I saw on TV once, a guy had to get his whole leg cut off just because he never treated a wound he got from a bike accident.

"Man, just get whatever alcohol you have. It'll have to do," I said to Noodles.

A few minutes later we were ready to baptize Needles in

Johnnie Walker. I took the towel and covered the mouth of the bottle. Then I turned it up, and back down, just to dampen it.

"This is gonna sting just a little, but I promise you, it'll help."

Needles wouldn't take his eyes off me. He never glanced at his brother, once. It was like Noodles wasn't even in the room anymore. Like he didn't exist. Looking Needles in the eye, I dabbed the rag on the first cut. He made a painful sizzling noise with his mouth. I knew the feeling—I did this every time I got a cut, but I always hollered. But my boy Needles took it like a man.

Then I checked to see if any bones were broken.

"Look, man, we can't take him to the hospital," Noodles said as I felt up and down Needles's arms and legs, searching for fractures or anything that seemed out of place. He was right. Nobody in our neighborhood could go to the hospital. A trip to the hospital could mean the end to a roof over your head. Can't pay hospital bills and rent. One time, this girl who used to live down the block, Sasha Lee, got hit by a car. I think I was around ten. The car hit her so hard, she flew up in the air and landed on the other side of the street. Everybody knew she was dead. She had to be. Her mother came flying down the block. We all ran over to help. By the time I got down the block, Ms. Lee had Sasha up and was half carrying, half dragging her aimlessly down the block, toward Lewis Ave. Somebody shouted, "Call the ambulance!" Ms. Lee quickly shouted, "No! No ambulance! She'll be okay. We'll catch a cab to the clinic tomorrow."

So, yeah, I was praying that none of Needles's bones were broken, because like Noodles said, we couldn't take him to the hospital.

"I know that. But we still gotta check," I explained.

I kept pinching at his joints, asking if this hurt or if that hurt, to all of which Needles shook his head no, until I got to his wrist. I pinched the two bones on the sides of his wrist. The ones that feel like marbles under the skin.

"Ah!" Needles cried out. He hissed and snatched his wrist away, that fast.

"Sorry, sorry," I said. "Nood, you got anything we can wrap his wrist with?"

At this point I didn't even know why I was asking. I knew he wouldn't be able to find anything, and I wouldn't be able to find anything either.

Still, Noodles ran out of the room to go search for something we could use as bandage.

Needles lay there cradling his wrist with his other hand. His eyes were swollen. He looked sad, angry, and uncomfortable all at the same time. But at least he looked a little more alert. "Needles, good news is, I don't think it's broken," I told him. "Probably just sprained. We'll just ice it." I forced a smile.

"Noodles, just get some ice!" I yelled.

He came back in the room with nothing but a frown on his face.

"No ice, Ali."

No ice. The house didn't even have frozen water. So I yanked one of Needles's socks off his foot, and wrapped it tight around his wrist. I didn't know what it would do, or if it would do anything at all, but it was all I could think of. "Can you at least find some aspirin?"

After I helped Needles swallow the aspirin, I stepped back and took one good look at him. He lay there like some sort of insect, maybe a slug with fresh salt poured on him, disintegrating slowly. Totally weird, but I couldn't help but think that his face looked like some kind of jigsaw puzzle, the pieces not quite in the right place. Lip swollen. Nose bloody. His eyes just starting to blacken and puff up. It was gonna be a long, hard night for Needles, which sucked because it had started so good.

I sat with him as he started to drift off, and began looking around his room. He never let anyone in it, and it was a total surprise—it was nothing like the rest of the house. It was bright, and the walls were covered in posters of old-school rappers from the nineties, and pictures of him and Noodles, and their mother looking a lot less tired than I'm used to seeing her, and a man I had never seen before, who I figured was their father, judging from how much they all looked alike. The place in the pictures definitely wasn't this apartment, that's for sure. Everybody looked happy. On top of all that, Needles's room was neat. Every shoe, every shirt, every little thing was in its place.

I glanced over at Noodles and thought about whether or not I should talk to him about what happened at the party. Then I realized I had to. But I didn't want to do it with Needles right there, even though I thought it would be the perfect opportunity for Needles to get some stuff off his own chest, if he only had the energy to talk. Shoot, all he really had to do was drop an F-bomb. Noodles would've got the message loud and clear. But Needles looked like he was falling asleep and was refusing to acknowledge his brother at all. It wasn't for me to force it. But it was my place to speak up about why I had to jump in and risk my own life when me and Needles ain't got no blood between us.

"Let's let him sleep," I whispered to Noodles, pointing toward the bedroom door. After softly closing it behind me, we went into the living room, where I sat down on the same nasty chair, with the stuffing on the seat part. I don't know why I even sat down. I should've been going home. My work was done. Needles was safe and almost asleep. But I sat, because if I walked out of that apartment, we would most likely never discuss what happened. It would never come up. It would get swept under the rug like so many of the other weird and strained parts of our friendship.

"Yo, man, what was all that about?" I said at last, assuming he would be able to pick up from the tone of my voice that I was talking about him not defending his brother at the party.

Noodles was leaning against the kitchen counter. The tired on his face was almost as bad as the sadness. I waited to see if he would get all cocky, let his ego take control of his tongue. I was ready for whatever "You don't know about me and my brother" trash he was about to try to kick to me.

"What was what about?" he said stupidly.

I sat there for a second to collect my thoughts. I didn't want to blow up.

"Hmmm. Let me think. Your brother was getting the crap beat out of him—four against ONE—and you were off in the corner, doing JACK! You moused up, man!"

Noodles's eyes welled up, and he hung his head. It was the first time I had ever seen him do that.

"I don't know what happened, man," he said finally.

Wrong answer. Think a little harder, I wanted to say.

"Aight. Well, let's start from the beginning. Why did they jump Needles? Last I checked, he was chilling in the corner, out of the way. So get me from point A to point Z, Noodles, because I'm really having a hard time understanding what the hell went wrong." Man, I sounded just like Doris. Point A to point Z. That was definitely Doris. Every time something happened in the house and neither Jazz or I wanted to rat the other person out, we would stall as best we could. That's when Doris would pull out the A to Z thing, and the way she said it made it seem like if we didn't get to point Z quickly, she was going to B, C, D, E, F, G, H, I, and J all up and down our butts. I wanted Noodles to feel that same threat. The threat of a Doris whooping, through the hands of her first-born. Me.

Noodles stared at the floor, which I didn't like. I did like the fact that he was now humble, but I didn't like the fact that he was acting like a chump. I wasn't his father or the police. I was his friend. Look me in my eye, so that I know whatever you are about to say is the truth.

"It was me," he said. His words came out like the squeak of a mouse caught on one of those nasty sticky pads.

"What was you?" God, Doris was all over me.

He raised his head, finally, like a man.

"He did it for me, Ali," Noodles blurted out, and then, to my horror, he started to whine. Not cry, just whine. "I was with Tasha almost the whole time, and everything was cool. So cool! I told her I would be right back because I had to run to the bathroom. So I started walking through the crowd, and some dude stepped on my foot. So—"

"Wait. Please don't tell me this is gonna be one of those 'Somebody stepped on my foot, so I had to fight him, because he smudged my shoe' stories."

"Just listen, man," Noodles pleaded. I could tell he really felt bad, so I just shut up and let him finish. But still, I hoped it wasn't one of those.

"So this dude, who was obviously wasted, stepped on my foot. Now, Ali, I knew what the deal was. You know that. I didn't want no parts of nobody in there because they were all older than us, plus, Tasha let us in, and I wasn't trying to get her in no trouble with MoMo. I promised her that. We all did. But Ali, my shoes were too small. My feet were killing me! So when that fool stepped on my foot, my reflex kicked in and I pushed him—just so that he would get off my foot—I swear! It hurt like crazy, my toes all bunched up in them shoes. And this fool wanna put his two-hundred-pound bear paw on it! It was like when you at the doctor's and they hit your knee with that hammer, and your leg kick out. Reflex."

I understood what Noodles was saying, but I wasn't letting him off the hook.

"Aight, and then what?"

"The first thing I did was apologize to the dude. Me, Ali! I said I was sorry. But then the dude got all wild on me. I don't know if he couldn't make out that I was saying I was sorry for pushing him, because of all the music blasting and people shouting, but I was. Next thing I knew, he just started snapping on me out of nowhere. Like, just barking on me. And I couldn't understand what he was saying exactly, but I knew he was mad. The people next to him were gassing him, telling him this and that, and I couldn't make out what they were saying either, but I could tell they were pumping this dude up. It was almost like he was looking for trouble. Like he was just trying to find the right foot to step on, the one in the too-small shoes.

"While all this is happening, I'm steady trying to cool homeboy down. I'm screaming that I didn't mean anything, and that it was a reflex and not personal. But his goons are all around him, still hyping the whole situation. Then he pushed me. I mean, it felt like he was trying to put both of his hands through my chest. I stumbled back and fell on some other drunk dude, who then started popping off at the mouth too. At me! I didn't even do nothing to that dude, but he ain't care. He was pissed at me for falling into him. I tried to explain that the other guy pushed me, but he wasn't hearing it.

"So here I am between these two drunk beasts who look crazy enough to head-butt me, or bite me, or something wild like that. The kinda dudes who don't play by no rules."

"So why didn't you just roll out?" I asked.

"I tried. But as soon as I was about to, Needles showed up to see what was going on. The dudes instantly assumed that Needles was there to back me up and that now we were ready to rumble or something. Like my scrawny brother had come to save me."

"Maybe he did."

Noodles huffed to himself.

"Yeah, maybe he did," he conceded. "Anyway, so Needles is standing there with his yarn and all that, and I'm trying to explain to him what's going on as quickly as possible, as well as turn him so that we can sort of start at least trying to walk away from them, but when we took a step, the first guy grabbed me and spun me around." Here Noodles paused and looked me right in the eye. "Ali, as soon as I spun around, Needles had a tick."

"Oh no. Don't tell me . . ."

"Yep. He jerked, and jabbed one of his needles right into the dude's side!"

"Did it go in?"

"Man, I don't know. All I know is, dude started shouting something about Needles stabbing him, and then . . ."

Noodles stopped talking. It's like he couldn't say anything else. Like his throat closed up. And I felt a little bit bad for him . . . I really did. But then I kept seeing all those dudes beating poor Needles down, in my mind. And something bubbled up.

"And then you ran," I said plainly. I wasn't going to be

easy on him with all this. I had been too easy for too long. I remembered what my mother had said about getting tired of bailing people out. People in this case, being Noodles. I was definitely tired, like I had been carrying him on my back for miles, and all he ever did was dig his heels into my ribs like a jockey on a horse.

"How could you, Nood?" I felt like I didn't know him, because as far as I was concerned, I didn't. Or maybe I did. Maybe I knew him all too well. Maybe I knew exactly who he was, but I never wanted to admit it to myself, because he was my only real friend. I pledged my friendship, and in our neighborhood your word is your bond and loyalty is everything. But Noodles hadn't been loyal, had he? I mean, he turned his back on his own brother. What if it was me being jumped?

I glanced at the microwave: 9:27. I knew that was wrong. It figures that they wouldn't set the clock. I patted my pockets for my cell phone to check the time. That's when I realized my phone was missing. Damn. I must have lost it in the fight.

I stood up. It was time for me to go. I didn't know exactly what time it was, but I knew it was late, and I could have just asked Noodles to check his phone and tell me, but I felt like if I opened my mouth to ask him anything, it would be followed up with my fist.

"Where you going?" Noodles asked, as if I didn't have a home to go to. As if I owed him something. I didn't answer. I just headed toward the door.

"Wait, Ali!"

I kept walking.

"Ali!"

The space between the raggedy chair and card table and the door seemed like the length of a football field, and I was running slowly toward the end zone trying not to let Noodles's words run me down and tackle me. I couldn't let them. Not tonight. Not after what happened.

"Ali!" he screamed, loud enough to startle me. I turned around and gave him a cold stare without saying a word.

"It's because our father left when he heard that Needles had a syndrome."

I was confused. "Nood, honestly, I don't know what you're talking about, and tonight I don't think I care."

"Ali—I ain't seen him in years. He bounced way before we moved around here." Noodles's voice started cracking. "Everything was cool, but as soon as the syndrome started, he was out. He ain't want no kid with no syndrome. He figured Needles was crazy, so eventually I might be too, and we would make him look bad. This is what my mother told me. She said, when the doctors said Needles had the syndrome, my father was so mad that he punched a hole in the wall. I don't remember that, but the next morning he was gone."

I still stood there, emotionless.

"That's why—that's why I'm so hard on him." Noodles started looking glassy. "If he ain't have that stupid syndrome, we'd still have a father. We'd still have a family. It changed everything. Ma got all depressed, and down, and started staying out all late with strangers, and coming in looking all beat-up and old. We had to move to this crappy apartment, with crack-heads running around upstairs. Everything was ruined. And I know it ain't Needles's fault, Ali. I know it ain't, but . . ."

His voice was cracking, and I could tell he was holding back his tears, literally shaking, trying not to cry. I stood there unable to give him any of the support I guess he expected me to give. But I appreciated him finally answering the question that I asked him earlier, and could even respect him for coming to grips with the fact that it's not Needles's fault that he has a syndrome, and that they don't have a father. I still couldn't find nothing nice to say to Noodles to make him feel better, though. There was no hug in me—he had emptied me out. I couldn't do nothing else to try to help him. So I turned around, and left.

The moment I turned the knob to my front door, pain shot through my fingertips. I'd been so worried about Needles that I had forgotten that my hand was messed up! The pain was sharp, like little lightning bolts striking under my skin, hitting every nerve. I almost cried out, but I held it together. I couldn't make too much noise. My mother and sister were asleep, and I needed to slip into bed as quietly and as cool as possible. Didn't want to wake anyone and then have to explain my busted lip, or why I'm home so late. Funny thing is, I didn't even know what time it was, but I knew it was definitely past curfew. I took my shoes off at the door. They were no longer clean and white. No longer perfect. In fact, they were a clear sign of how the night had gone—all wrong. Filthy. Little splats of blood on the left one. I wasn't sure whose it was, but I hoped it wasn't mine. The shoes were ruined, and I thought, darkly, that they would definitely be a reminder. A symbol of what protection and loyalty looks like. And in some screwed-up way, my first real victory. Hell, my first real fight! I would keep them, I thought. At least the left one. Definitely the left one.

I slid my feet across the floor, like a forward moonwalk, past the couch and television and down the hall into my room. I put my shoes as far under the bed as I could, then took off the rest of my clothes. Only then did I go to the bathroom to see how bad my face was. I was only hit a few times, so I didn't think there would be too much damage. I flipped the light switch in the bathroom. The buzzing fan kicked in, and I stared in the mirror. The one sign of me being tagged was my lip, which was a little swollen, mainly on the inside. That would go down by the morning. My jaw felt stiff, so I opened and closed my mouth like I was chewing on Silly Putty or cheap bodega candy. Lemonheads, Laffy Taffy. I could hear the hinge of my jaw clicking every time I opened my mouth, but I knew it would be fine. Wasn't the first time. I had taken one to the jaw a few times before, messing around with Malloy, enough that it's gotten pretty sturdy over the last few years.

I washed my hands, splashed water on my face, and slipped back into my bedroom. My mattress, old and lumpy, was now a small piece of paradise, right there in my room. It never felt so good to be home. Crazy as it sounds, I had never been so excited to go to bed. I lay there for a moment and thought about all that had happened.

Suddenly it all came crashing down on me. The pain. My jaw. My hand. My mom's advice, now ringing in my head, about when I can't do it anymore, when I can't put up with Noodles and his crap, I'll know it. And I knew it. I mean, I was his friend, but was he mine? Did he even know how to be a friend? How to be a brother? Maybe he didn't mean any harm, and couldn't control himself—like a different kind of syndrome. Or better yet, maybe he was just a selfish poseur, using his daddy as an excuse to be wack. Just thinking about it started pissing me off all over again, so I decided to try to go to sleep.

I couldn't have had my eyes closed for more than five minutes before I heard a noise coming from the living room. At first I thought it was a mouse, which was no big deal. Mice might as well pay rent around here. That's what the old folks always say. But then I heard the noise again. It was louder. It sounded like someone scratching at the door, fidgeting with something they shouldn't have been fidgeting with—the lock. Now, unless this was a mouse the size of a bear, someone was trying to break into our apartment! I sat straight up in the bed so I could hear better. My mouth instantly got dry, and my heart started pounding hard enough to bust. Break-ins don't really happen much around here, because it's too hard to get into a brownstone. Way too many doors and steps just to get a TV and a couple pieces of jewelry. So usually when someone's house gets broken into, it's not to steal. It's to get someone.

And then it hit me. Could it be the dudes from MoMo's party? Naw. I mean, nobody knows where I live. At least I don't think so. Except MoMo. But he didn't see me. Or did he? But he wouldn't tell those goons where I stay, and put me and my family in danger, right? Right?

The lumps in the mattress seemed to get harder, and my

pillow all of a sudden felt like a concrete slab. Everything was uncomfortable again as my nerves shook off the sleep. Part of me wanted to close my eyes and become Noodles, scared and disconnected, hiding in a corner hoping a superhero would come save me. But just like at the party, I didn't have time to be scared. Well, I take that back. I was scared, but I still had to do something. Especially since my mom and my little sister were right across the hall, asleep. All I could do is hope that whoever was coming to get me didn't have a gun. Please don't have a gun!

I reached under my bed and got the baseball bat my father gave me years ago. He was a big believer of having a bat under the bed to protect the family, just in case. Now just in case was happening. I slipped out of bed again, this time being extra sure to make no sound at all. I started creeping through the hall, the bat clinched tight in my right hand, my left hand sliding softly along the wall to guide me. Yeah, my heart was pounding hard enough to explode, but I forced myself to be a ninja.

I could still hear the lock being picked. Whoever was out there was trying to open it as slowly and carefully as possible, and was taking their time, trying not to wake anyone. Well, I was awake—I'd never actually felt more awake—and ready to put whoever was behind the door straight to sleep. Well, not really. All I was expecting to do was just smash his hand whenever he tried to undo the chain lock. But then I realized, I forgot to put the stupid chain on the door! Stupid, stupid, STUPID!

Suddenly the knob turned. Now, like I said, I was scared, but I felt kinda pumped up too, like at the party. No one was getting into my house. I would wait for whoever it was to come in, and then try to take his head off.

The person pushed the door open, slowly, just enough for his slim, slimy self to creep in. I stood just to the right of the door. He couldn't see me because he slid in on the left, of course.

On three, aim for his face. One. Two. Three. Right when I started swinging the bat, the light flipped on. I was blinded by the sudden flash in the room, but I knew I connected.

"Jesus Christ!" he screamed. "Are you crazy, Ali!"

The voice was instantly familiar.

It was my father.

I gasped, and blinked madly, trying to see in the light. He was holding the side of his mouth. "What the hell are you doing?" he shouted, yanking the bat from me. And then he said, "And what are you doing, Doris?"

I turned around, and there she was, my mother, standing in the hall with a faded pink, oversize T-shirt, QUEENS SLEEP ALONE across the front in a corny cursive. She was holding the biggest knife I had ever seen. It definitely wasn't the one Jazz chops onions with, that's for sure.

"I heard something," she said. She stood there shocked and scared, but ready nonetheless. I guess she was going to protect me while I was protecting her. The whole thing was kinda absurd, and my heartbeat started getting back to normal.

"What are you doing, John?" Doris said back to my father. Then she added with her familiar bite, "Why you breaking in this time of night?" As if there was a better time to be "breaking in."

"Breaking in? I have a key, remember? I was trying to be quiet. Was just gonna come in, check on this fool, then leave." John shot me a look. He was opening and closing his mouth like I had been earlier. I wondered if his jaw was clicking. The bat must've caught him pretty clean.

"Check on him for what?" Now Doris shot me a look.

Shoot. I totally forgot, I was supposed to text him when I got in. But I wouldn't have been able to do it anyway because I didn't have my phone. Damn! Damn, damn, damn! I looked at John, hoping that he could see in my eyes that I needed him to cover for me.

He shifted his eyes from mine, and I already knew what was coming, but I still tried to stall.

"Yeah, check on me for what?" I asked nervously.

"Ali, please. You broke the rules. We had a deal," he said, pushing past me. He took a seat on the couch and massaged his jaw.

"What is going on?" my mother demanded. I couldn't tell if she was worried, or if she was just wondering why my father had plopped down on the sofa like he was planning to stay awhile.

"You want me to tell her, or will you do the honors like a man, son?" My father looked at me with a butthole look on his face. The kind of look that burns me up on the inside.

He used that "like a man" all the time to trick me into telling on myself, but it was okay, because I did believe that a man stands up and admits what he's done. A man takes the heat coming to him. But I just wasn't ready for it yet.

"She already knew," I said. I figured it was worth a shot.

"Knew what?" my mother asked.

"That I was hanging out with Needles and Noodles."

Doris nodded her head. John shook his.

"Oh, so your mother knew you and Needles and Noodles—"

"Okay, okay, I'll tell her!" I cut him off, talking in a much higher pitch than normal.

"Tell me what? What's going on!" Doris yelped, frustrated. I could tell she was getting nervous. She took a seat on the couch next to John. He scootched over just a little, just enough to keep their legs touching. She didn't look uncomfortable but not really comfortable, either. Somewhere right in the middle. Well, mainly she looked pissed. She probably wasn't even thinking about John.

"I went out tonight."

"Ali!" John barked. That's all. Just "Ali!" I knew what that meant. That meant, get to the point before he got to the point for me. It's funny how his fatherhood kicked in at the most inconvenient times.

"Okay, okay!" I snapped. "Ma, I went to a party." I paused, and my father glared at me. "A MoMo party," I added.

My mother looked at John, confused.

"What the hell is a MoMo?" she asked. I wanted to laugh, but I knew that would've got me popped.

"MoMo, Doris. Maurice Williams, from down the other side of Lewis. Thomas and Greta's boy. He has these parties and—" John stopped. Looked at me. "Matter fact, I'm just gonna let Ali here tell you about the parties."

My mother looked up at me, her eyes big but tired, waiting for whatever disappointing blow was about to come through my lips. I took a deep breath. Who would've thought it'd be so hard to swallow air?

"MoMo has these parties. And usually no one is allowed unless you are eighteen or older. But I got invited."

Doris cut me off. "By who?" She sat ramrod straight and looked like she was either correcting bad posture or avoiding getting too comfortable next to John.

My mind was racing. I knew I couldn't snitch on Tasha. If I said Tasha invited me, then my mother would've asked what a young girl like Tasha was doing there, and if MoMo and Tasha's parents knew, and that if they didn't, she would, of course, have to tell them because she's a parent and she knows what it's like to try to keep kids out of trouble, and then Tasha would be angry with me and surely never talk to me again, even though that was already a possibility because I beat the brakes off her brother's friends.

"By MoMo," I heard myself say. I sucked as a liar.

"By MoMo? Why would he invite you, a minor, to his party, Ali?" She looked at me sideways. I mean, she literally turned her head to the side and looked me up and down, as if seeing me from the sideways angle would help her better see the lie. Or maybe she knew that it would help me to better see that I was caught, and that the lying better stop instantly.

I tried to catch John's eye. I knew he knew why I had to lie. I silently begged him for a little help, just to throw me one more bone to not get this girl, my friend Tasha, who I already let down, in trouble.

"What you scared of, Ali?" John asked. He could tell I was holding back for a reason.

"Man, I can't snitch," I said, tough. Well, that got my mother all worked up, antsy like the cushion she was sitting on got hot. She started shaking her head and rocking back and forth like the junkies do on Fulton.

John sat there for a second. He wiped some of the tired off his face.

"I understand," he said. "Word is bond. I ain't no snitch neither."

"What's that supposed to mean?" Doris demanded.

"That means that what he tells me—us—stays right here in this room, got me?" He nodded his head at Doris to make sure she understood.

It felt good to know that John had come back to cool. All that foot-putting-down wasn't hitting on nothing.

"Okay," I said, feeling like maybe I could breathe again. "Tasha invited us."

"Who exactly is us?" my mother asked. Then she thought about it. "No, wait, let me guess. That Noodles went too, didn't he?" Whenever something went wrong, he was that Noodles.

"Yeah, but Needles was with us too," I said quickly, hoping that Needles's name would soften the blow, since she had a soft spot for him.

"Needles! Lord! Y'all dragged that sweet child into y'all's mess? Y'all really are something," she fumed, looking at John, shaking her head. "And exactly what happened at this party, Ali?" I swear, my mother was getting her TV lawyer on.

"Nothing. We partied," I said. Short and to the point.

"Nothing?" Doris said, once again looking at me sideways.

"Nothing?" John followed up like a bratty little sister playing copycat.

"I mean, not nothing. Something happened. But nothing to be worried about. Everything is cool," I quickly assured them.

My father, his eyes squinting, was now taking in my split lip, I could tell. But instead he asked, "What happened to your hand?"

I looked down, and I couldn't believe it—it was swollen twice its normal size. It had blown up like a balloon animal.

"Jesus Christ, what happened!" my mother shrieked, jumping to her feet. She took up my hurt hand and compared it with the other one.

"What happened?" she asked again, this time her voice gentler, more worried. "And I want the truth, Ali! No more beating around the bush!"

So, I laid it out.

"Okay, the truth," I started. I winced as my mother softly pressed at each finger, which, believe me, did *not* feel good.

My father leaned forward just to make it clear that he was listening as well. I knew part of him wanted to hear this story for no other reason than the fact that it was juicy. He was funny in that way. Immature sometimes but cool about it.

"We went to the party because Tasha works the door, so she let us in. When we got there, everything was chill. Just music, food, drinks, and a bunch of people."

"What kind of people, son?" My mother closed her eyes when she asked that. It's what she did when she was getting upset.

"All kinds. Lots of girls—well, women, and lots of dudes who seemed to have money. I only say that because of the clothes they were wearing. But I could be wrong, they all might live at home like me, and just borrowed clothes from their homeboys or their fa—"

"Ali!" John said, pissed. I realized I almost slipped.

My mother spun around toward him. "Wait a minute. You knew, didn't you! You knew he was going to that party. That's why you were checking on him!"

"Don't be mad at him, Ma," I begged. "None of this is his fault!"

She stared up at the ceiling for a second, then turned back toward me. "Ali, I ain't got enough mad for both of y'all, so since you my responsibility, I'm gonna save all the mad for you. And now you're going to tell me exactly what happened."

"Okay. So we're there, and after a while the three of us split up. Noodles was close to the door talking to Tasha.

Needles was in the corner with his yarn, knitting and staying clear from any trouble. And I was just dancing around, doing my thing or whatever."

"Get to the point, Ali!" Doris barked.

"Okay, okay! So, long story short, Noodles had gotten into a stupid confrontation that really wasn't his fault. Some guys were trying to chump him. So then Needles comes over to see what's going on and ends up stabbing one of the dudes with one of his knitting needles."

"He what?" my mom gasped.

"On purpose?" John asked.

"No, fool. Needles wouldn't do that," Doris insisted.

"He has ticks sometimes," I reminded my dad. "Y'all seen it, when his arms jerk out. Noodles said that's what he thinks happened. Either way, Needles was trying to protect his brother, and that's all that really matters.

"Of course, after that they start jumping Needles, and Noodles punked out and ran, so I had no choice but to jump in it. And that's really it. I mean, I don't know what else to say."

I felt kind of embarrassed all of a sudden.

By now my mother had one hand over her mouth and the other fanning back the tears in her eyes. My father was gently rubbing her back.

"I had to. They would've killed him, Ma. I swear."

The tears started coming down my mother's cheeks, and she started trembling like a child on the first day of the flu. She wanted to say something, but she couldn't speak. Doris is a tough woman, but she did not do well with violence and fighting. She wasn't even too cool with the fact that I had been boxing all these years, but let it slide because I got to be around Malloy. Plus she knew I was too scared to have a real match anyway. Violence just wasn't her thing, especially when it came to either of her kids, or good, genuine people like Needles. And I don't mean special in the sense of mentally ill, I mean special in the sense of good, genuine people, and that's definitely Needles.

My father stood up. He seemed taller, more like a parent.

"Man to man," he started, "did you handle yourself?"

I knew what he meant. He knew fighting had never really come easy for me, and wanted to know if I made those guys pay. It's a question that I'm sure my mother wanted to know too, but she'd have never asked.

Without going into detail, I answered, "Yeah."

He nodded his head and put his hand on my shoulder, squeezing it enough to tell me that I had done the right thing and that he was proud. My mother sank back down on the couch. John walked over to the kitchen and began to fill a few glasses of water.

I sat down next to my mom. I felt terrible. Really terrible. She was totally upset, and it was my fault. Now I didn't know whether to hug her or just ask her to dismiss me.

She pressed her thumb against her eyes and took the water that John brought her. He stood to the side and gulped down his own glass, each swallow oddly loud.

"Is . . . ," she started, stopped, then started again. "Is Needles all right?"

"Yeah. He's beat pretty bad, but he's okay. I got him home and took care of him."

She nodded and flashed me a half smile. That smile let me know that she was mad at me for going but happy I took care of my friend. That I did what they taught me to do, take care of the folks I love. I could tell Doris knew I did what I had to do. So, feeling like she wasn't too too mad, I laid my head on her shoulder.

She drank the rest of the water, and after a few seconds she bounced her shoulder just enough for my head to pop up.

"You know you in trouble, right? I mean, grounded. Big-time. We'll talk about it tomorrow," she said, her voice suddenly calm. Sleep was all over the room. We were all exhausted. John was leaning against the wall like a zombie.

"And maybe have Malloy look at that hand tomorrow too, if your mother lets you out," John suggested.

I didn't say anything. Just nodded and made my way back to bed.

★ 12 ★

The next morning I woke up later than usual, probably because I hadn't gone to sleep until four in the morning. My face felt heavy, sore, and I knew that there would probably be a bruise. I was in no hurry to rush to the bathroom to see it; I knew it was there. I could feel the blue color. I held my hand in front of my face. It looked like one of those big foam hands you get when you go see the Yankees or the Knicks, except it was stiff and throbbing. I've never seen either of them live—the Yankees or the Knicks—but I've seen those hands on TV enough. John always said he'd take me and Jazz to get one, but never did. I don't think it's because he didn't want to. I just don't think he could ever afford it.

I eased out of bed like an old man, my body cramped and stubborn. The TV in the living room was buzzing with its usual "You are not the father." Jazz was having her daily coffee in the form of trash talk shows. I could smell that she had cooked. Bacon. Eggs. French toast maybe. But my smelling breakfast was interrupted by my suddenly wondering whether or not I was going to tell Jazz what happened last night. I knew she'd wonder why I was staying in the house all day, which I surely would be, for who knows how long. Maybe I would tell her I just wanted to spend some time with her. But she ain't dumb. Plus she'd notice my swollen hand and bruised-up face and have a heart attack, and go right into mother role, trying to ice it, heat it, wrap it. I'd look like a mummy when she got through with me.

I would have to tell her then. But I knew she wouldn't do well with news that I got into a fight, and that Needles got beaten pretty bad. So maybe I'd leave that part out, the part about Needles. No matter how old she acted, some things were still too much for her. Doris could barely take the news, so I knew Jazz would be crushed. So I decided to just not say anything at all about it, then shoot from the hip when she started asking questions.

The light from the hallway blinded me for a second. I thought about how this must be what it's like to go to heaven—walking toward the blinding light, with the smell of bacon and eggs all around. Jazz was jumping from the talk shows to the news and back to the talk shows. It was all so predictable.

The floor creaked.

"Ali?" Jazz called, sort of excited.

Just the sound of her saying my name made my eyes water. I don't know why, but it did.

"Yeah," I said, turning the corner so she could see me.

She, hopped off the couch and ran toward me, almost tripping over her oversize socks, my socks, dragging behind her like two tails on her feet. She threw herself at me, wrapping her arms tight around my waist and squeezing as hard as she could, which wasn't very hard, but hard enough for me to be reminded again that I had been fighting the night before.

"You okay?" she asked me, her head pressed against my chest.

"Of course. Why?" Why was she asking me this?

She pulled away so that I could see her face. This morning she looked innocent. No grown woman stuff. No old soul-ness. She looked eleven.

"Y'all were making so much noise last night, I couldn't sleep," she said. I felt my heart drop to my knees. "I wasn't listening, Ali, but I could hear, y'know?"

Now her little face was all tensed up. This is why I didn't want her to know about this. Another layer of guilt came over me.

"Let's sit down," I said, taking her hand, walking her back over to the couch. "I'm fine. Everyone is fine, Jazz."

"Even Needles?"

"Even Needles." At least I hoped so.

Jazz wiped a tear from her cheek, but more kept rolling down. She grabbed a napkin from the table, where two plates were set, both empty, except for crumbs of bacon and bread dust.

"Dang, Jazz, did I sleep too late? You ate mine and yours?" I asked, laughing, trying to lighten the mood.

"No, man," she said, looking at me more like her usual young-old self. "When I came out here this morning, Dad was knocked out on the couch. So I made him a plate."

"Dad?"

My dad hasn't slept here since . . . I don't even remember the last time! For Doris to actually let him stay was big. I mean, it was late and all, but still. My mother is the type of woman who, once she puts her foot down, it's down, no matter how late it is. It wouldn't have surprised me at all if she sent him packing in the middle of the night. But she didn't.

"Yep. He was laid out just like a little baby. I couldn't believe it."

"And where was Mom?" I tried to hold in a smile.

"Where she always is. Work."

To wake up to John asleep in our house must've been like Christmas for Jazz. She didn't tell me this, but I know she ran and jumped on him, and kissed his face, and played tickle monster, and hugged him like she hugged me earlier, but ten times tighter. I wish I had seen it.

"That bruise is nasty, Ali." Jazz reached up but kept herself from touching it at the last second. "And let me see that hand y'all were talking about last night."

I lifted it. Then I lifted the other one so that she could compare.

Her mouth dropped.

"Yeah, pretty gross, right?"

Jazz got a foul look on her face and turned away. I'm sure she regretted asking to see it.

"I did fix you a plate, by the way. Don't want you to get jealous," she joked, clearly trying to take her mind away from my giant hand. "It's in the microwave."

On the counter, right by the microwave, lay a sheet of torn-out notebook paper. In black marker was written:

PUNISHMENT! You are NOT allowed to
leave the house, except to go get your hand
looked at by Malloy. I know you're supposed
to work for him today, but I HAVE
ALREADY SPOKEN TO HIM. YOU CAN
ONLY STAY THERE FOR 30 MINUTES,
FOR HIM TO FINISH YOUR HAND,
THEN COME STRAIGHT BACK HOME!
I AM NOT PLAYING WITH YOU, ALI.
In the house I need you to give the bathroom
some love, as well as the kitchen, living
room, and your bedroom. DUST, SWEEP,
MOP, AND CLEAN EVERYTHING!
AGAIN, I AM NOT PLAYING WITH
YOU. DO NOT TEST ME, ALI.

And then, after all that, it said, "I love you, son," and was signed, "Your mother."

I couldn't even be upset about it because I knew it was coming. And it actually wasn't as bad as I thought it was going to be. I took the food out of the microwave and scarfed it down using my left hand, which was weird, but my right hand couldn't even hold a fork. Then I downed two aspirin with orange juice, gave Jazz a kiss on the cheek, and headed out to Malloy's.

★ 13 ★

It's funny to think about how fast things change. A day ago I was regular Ali, throwing jabs in the shower and shadow-boxing my own reflection in my mother's mirror. Most people around here didn't even know about me training at Malloy's for years, punching the bag, and learning how to snap my jab and move my feet. And even though over time I got pretty good, I still wasn't brave enough to ever really fight anyone. Just didn't think it was in me. But after MoMo's party I was sure half the hood thought I was some gladiator. Shoot, I kinda thought so too! And now I had to march down to Malloy's house with my giant hand and tell him what happened.

When I got there, I knocked on the door, but it was open, so the first knock opened it more.

"Malloy? You in there?"

"Yeah, I'm in here," his voice, sluggish and scratchy, came from inside. I could smell the cigarettes and musky liquor breath from outside.

"Well, well, well, my man Muhammad Ali is in the house! Heard you taking jokers down for the count!" he said, but not smiling or laughing, or showing any signs of it being a joke.

I leaned against the wall, deflated. Part of me wanted him to know how bad I, Allen Brooks, whooped those dudes, but another part of me was embarrassed about the whole thing.

"Even if your mother hadn't told me, I would've found out," he explained. "This is Decatur Street, son. Bed-Stuy, Brooklyn. The streets talk anyway, but they talk even louder to me," he said like a big shot. The Newport dangled from his lip, the ash ready to fall onto his leg. Luckily, those old-school jeans are too thick to burn, I thought.

I stood there, mute.

"So you gonna tell me about it? Or you just came to talk about girls?" Malloy said, still with no smile.

I smirked.

"I mean, ain't much to tell," I started. "I was at a party that I had to go to, but shouldn't have been at, and these guys start jumping Needles. So, I did what I had to do."

Malloy dabbed the cigarette out on the bare table. Then he tapped the Newport box for another.

"I see," he said, striking a match. "And where was his big, bad brother?"

I frowned. Just the thought of Noodles and what he did, or rather what he didn't do, made the skin on my face heavy. A frown was all I could show.

"He just stood there, scared, watching it all go down."

Malloy took a long long long drag on the cigarette, turning

half of it instantly to ash. He held it in for a moment, then blew the smoke toward the ceiling.

"Is that right?" he said. I hate when old people say that. Because they usually only say it because it's better than saying, duhhh, or I told you so. For Malloy, it was more like, duh. He never really talked too much about Noodles. He knew who he was, everyone did, and he knew he was my closest friend, which is why I think he kept whatever he felt about Noodles to himself. I appreciated that. But the one thing he had said was that I could never bring Noodles to his house to learn to box. He'd said, Noodles wasn't the kind of kid he wanted to teach something like boxing. Too much anger.

"Yeah. He just stood there." I felt kinda sick saying that— weird, like I was ratting Noodles out.

Malloy shook his head. "Well, let me tell you something." He crushed the cigarette under his fingers and started wheeling across the room. There was a little box on the other side. It looked like a plastic toolbox, but it was full of boxing stuff—tape, gauze, Vaseline, scissors. He took the gauze and the tape out, then wheeled over to me.

"Hand out," he said. I stretched my arm so he could see my hand. He took his thumb and pressed it gently along the knuckles. Fireworks went off up my arm.

"Hairline. Nothing too crazy. I'll wrap it. It'll heal itself." Malloy started unraveling the gauze. He put one end of it on the top of my hand, and pressed his finger down to hold the end in place until he wrapped the gauze around enough times to trap it down. I could tell he had done this tons of times.

"Let me tell you, son, punching bags don't punch back. But sometimes, when you take them for granted, and you get cocky, you can really hurt yourself when you punch one." Malloy wrapped the gauze in between my fingers and around my hand tightly. "Now, with them brothers, Needles and Noodles, who you think the punching bag is?"

I knew there was a point to this story, so I figured I'd better play along to get to it.

I thought for a second. Malloy started wrapping tape around the white cloth.

"Uh, I guess Needles?"

"Exactly. But who ends up hurt for taking Needles, the punching bag, for granted?"

"Noodles," I said confidently. Though I knew the answer, it wasn't exactly a lightbulb moment where I understood automatically what Malloy was talking about. I never did. At least not right away.

I let it sink in while Malloy ripped the white tape with his teeth.

"That'll do it," he said. "Next time, close your fist tight. You know that. Try to squeeze water out a rock. Got me?"

I nodded my head and resisted rolling my eyes.

"Now, do us both a favor, and go on home. Your mother told me thirty minutes, and we just hit thirty-two. So you gotta roll, 'cause Doris worse than a bomb in Vietnam, or a stiff jab from Ali. And by Ali, I mean you, my man." Malloy smiled just enough to let me know he was proud of me for facing my fear and fighting, even though it was a jacked-up situation. He wheeled backward to his table and grabbed his bottle and cup. He coughed mean and violent, and spit something thick into an old handkerchief he had tucked in his shirt pocket. Then he pulled twenty dollars, which would've been my pay for the day had I worked, from the same pocket. He held it up like he was going to give it to me anyway. As soon as I took a step toward him to grab it, he slipped it back in his shirt pocket, shook his head, and cracked a joke.

"You ain't work today, so if you want this, you gotta come fight for it, and this time in the ring, tough guy." He smiled and reached for his cigarettes. He just never let up.

I shook my head and let myself out.

★ 14 ★

The punching bag don't punch back. But you can hurt yourself when you punch one, if you take it for granted. Needles is the punching bag. Noodles is the puncher. But you can hurt yourself when you punch one. If you take it for granted. Needles is the punching bag. Noodles is the puncher. Needles, punching bag. Noodles, puncher.

I strolled down Decatur, back toward my house, thinking about what Malloy said. I walked at a medium pace. Not too fast. I had to spend the rest of the day inside, so there was no point in rushing back to my apartment prison. But not too slow, either. Doris was known for having spies on the block, clocking my every move whenever I was on punishment. If it looked like I was stalling, the neighbors would snitch, and she'd jump down my throat and tack on another week for lollygagging.

When I got to Needles and Noodles's house, I glanced over at the stoop. No one was there, which was rare. One of them was always sitting out there. But on this day the stoop had no stoopers. Or as my mother called us sometimes, stoopids.

I looked up at their window, the one in the kitchen. One of those cheap plastic white fans sat on the sill, spinning, circulating hot air from outside, inside, and from inside back out. I wondered what they were doing in there. Was Needles okay? Was Noodles looking after him, making sure the swelling was going down, and keeping that sprained wrist stable? I hoped so. Was he reading Needles comics, maybe? Were they talking? Had Noodles said he was sorry for being a punk and letting his brother take a beating? Maybe I should just go check on Needles to make sure everything was cool, I thought. But I really didn't want to see Noodles. At all. So, I kept on walking.

Once I got back in the house, Jazz was sitting right where I'd left her, sunken deep into the couch. Her legs were tucked under her, which always seemed like the most uncomfortable position to me. The TV was on, but now she was busy flipping through magazines and cutting out old photos, working on her scrapbook.

Eric, you are NOT the father!

Jazz never looked up but shook her head and tightened the sides of her mouth, just like our mother does whenever she thinks something is ridiculous. If Jazz wasn't Jazz, and was old enough to cuss, this look would be followed by "That's a damn shame" or something like that. That's what Doris always says.

The smell of breakfast was now overpowered by the suffocating but fresh smell of ammonia and bleach.

"Stink in here," I said, walking behind the couch. I rested the hand that wasn't all wrapped on one of Jazz's skinny brown shoulders. She had glued a picture of Doris and John onto a Jamaican cruise ad.

"I know." She tilted her head back. "I cleaned everything up for you."

"What you mean?"

Jazz slid her hand between the couch cushions and pulled out a crumpled piece of paper and held it up in the air so I could grab it. She grinned. It was the note Doris had left for me with my punishment on it. Jazz had checked off every assignment she had done. Bathroom. Check. Kitchen. Check. Living room. Check. Bedroom. No check there. She knew better than to go into my bedroom. Dust, sweep, mop. Check, check, and check.

I wanted to ask her why she did it, but I didn't because I already knew what she would say. She would say something about being my sister, and that it's no big deal, or something like that. Then she would've cracked a joke about it taking me a million hours to do forty-five minutes' worth of work, which is why Doris assigned it to me. Doris would never ask Jazz to do anything like this for a punishment. A punishment for Jazz would be more like keeping her from watching TV. Something like that. But this kind of stuff, house chores, was nothing to her.

I leaned down and kissed her on top of her head for the second time this morning.

"You said the living room was clean too, right?"

"Uh. Yeah," she said.

"But it ain't."

She glared at me.

"What you mean, it ain't?"

"Your dirty butt still in here," I said, laughing.

Jazz jumped up and stood on the couch, play-swinging her arms at me all wild for my face. My reflex kicked in, and I blocked her hand with mine, but I used the wrong hand. The fractured one. A bomb blew up in my knuckle that I could feel in my elbow, and then in my neck. It was like an exploding train traveling through a subway tunnel, on fire, and the last stop was right under my chin.

I jumped back in pain and started bouncing up and down and flicking my hand like Michael Jackson. I sucked air in between my teeth, making that hissing noise that people make whenever they are in pain but don't want to yell. I didn't want to yell. I knew Jazz didn't mean it. We were playing. She looked at me, frightened and guilty.

"I'm so sorry, Ali. It wasn't on purpose."

"I know, Jazz. I'm okay, I'm okay," I whispered, crouching down like someone had punched me in the stomach. Jazz rubbed my back and kept apologizing while the sting slowly drifted away. She felt so bad.

"Listen, if scrapbooking don't work out, you can always take up scrapping," I joked to make her feel better. "You hit hard!"

Jazz smirked. "Whatever. Shoulda never called me dirty."

"Oh yeah?" I straightened up and flashed a slick grin. "But you are dirty!"

Jazz sprung up, ready to swing again. I pretended to be scared and broke out running down the hall.

Around 5:15 Doris came home. I was in my bedroom straightening up things, shooting left-hand jumpers with pieces of trash into my garbage can on the other side of the room. Kobe or LeBron, ten seconds left, fourth quarter, game seven of the finals. Or like John would say, Air Jordan time. But when I heard Doris come in, I called a timeout and started making up my bed.

She poked her head in the room, looked at me, then at my hand and saw it was wrapped, shook her head, closed the door, and headed off to job number two. No speaking. That was her way of saying she was still kinda pissed about everything but not really pissed. If she was really pissed, then the tongue-lashing would've started again. Round two. She was famous for remembering something that she forgot to yell at you earlier, and dropping the wrath right back on you.

Around 5:45 John came in.

"Ali!" he yelled from the living room.

When I got there, Black was sitting on the couch next to Jazz, and John was leaning on the arm of the sofa.

"Hey," I said, sort of confused as to why Black was in our house. I gave him a pound. "Wassup, man."

"Sup, Ali."

"Ali, you know Black, right?" my father asked.

Obviously. "Yeah. Why? Wassup?"

My father glanced at Jazz, who was pretending to watch TV, but she was really waiting to hear what was going on. John knew this, I knew this, and Black knew this.

"Jazz, could you excuse us for a second, sweetie? Go hang in your room just for a few minutes."

Jazz huffed, but she got up and headed toward the back.

"Close the door, and keep it shut, Jazz! You hear?"

"Yes," she grumbled, huffing louder.

I sat in Jazz's spot on the couch, and Black moved over to create some space between us. My father stayed put.

"Tell him, Black," my father said, like he was some sort of gang leader, and Black was one of his loyal goons.

"Ali, I was at Brother's today," Black started. I instantly thought about the fact that Black knows how to cut hair but apparently not his own. "And you know, I was sitting there getting a cut, when a couple of dudes came in looking crazy. All black and blue like they had just been in a car crash or something. There was another guy already in there who knew the two guys who came in. They all dapped up and started talking."

"Okay," I said, waiting for why I should care about any of this.

"They started talking about MoMo's party, Ali. They started talking about you—about y'all. But mainly about you."

It felt like a rock was all of a sudden stuck in my throat.

"How you know they was talking about me?"

"Come on, Ali. They were talking about how some kid

caught them slipping when they were jumping some other dude, and lumped them up, pretty much. And how now they needed to find him. At first I didn't know it was you because I had no idea that you could fight, not to mention, what would you be doing at a MoMo party? But then they started talking about how the dude they were jumping had yarn with him. Said when they first hit him, a ball of knitting yarn flew up in the air. The other dude they were talking to thought that was hilarious." He paused, then added, "Only one guy in this hood got yarn. Needles. And I peeped Noodles's card when y'all were at my house. Dude's all bark and no bite. I know he can't fight. That leaves one Musketeer. You. Sound right?"

I looked at him for a second, stunned. "Yeah."

"Brother heard all the crap they was talking, and he recognized the part about the yarn too. He told the dudes that if they was gonna talk that mess, they had to leave—that his shop wasn't no thug meet-up spot. The boys gave Brother a little lip on their way out, and when they were gone, Brother and I talked about it. He knew the dudes from when he used to have a shop over in Brownsville. He said they were pretty raw cats, man. No games, all business. Bad business. He said he knew it was you they were looking for too. Had to be. So, I called your pops."

I felt like I was choking, but I managed to say, "I didn't even know y'all knew each other."

After I said it, I realized that, yeah, it actually makes perfect sense that they know each other. They are pretty much in the same line of work. Hustling. Not drugs or anything like that. Just everything else. My father, clothes. And Black, ser-vices. Birds of a feather.

"So what now?" I must admit, the rock in my throat had now become a brick. And my heart had become the broken washing machine at the laundromat. The one that jumps all around and makes all that noise. And my stomach, the big dryer on spin cycle.

"Now I stay close," my father said, tough.

"What you mean, close?"

"Close. If you need to go anywhere around here, I go too. At least for today." John wiped his face and took off his Yankees hat. Not the one he gave me but another one, and set it on top of the TV.

"I'm punished today, anyway. But what about tomorrow?" I asked nervously. The situation had gotten real. Somebody was looking for me. Somebody older and far meaner. And even though I beat them with my fists, I knew why my dad was sticking close—they were coming back with fire.

John scratched his head. For the first time, I realized that his hair was thinning at the top. He very seldom took off his hat, if ever, so I had never noticed his scalp peeking through. He old, but not in an old man kind of way. Just older. More grown-up, which, I know, is weird to say about a middle-aged father.

"Tomorrow," John started, picking at his beard. "Tomorrow I'll take care of it."

Instantly, my mind shot back to John's car. Not all the expensive clothes in the three suitcases in the trunk. Not the blanket or the cup with the toothbrush in it. Not the duffel bag with his knickknacks and Yankees hat in it. But that gun. The gun handle I saw sticking up, jammed between the driver's seat and the middle console. That handle was now knocking against my mind, like an angry fist on a wooden door.

I wanted to ask him what that meant—I'll take care of it—but I've learned over the years dealing with Doris that sometimes it's best to not ask. Sometimes you just got to keep your mouth shut. Something told me that this was one of those times, even though it was scaring the hell out of me.

We heard the creak of Jazz's door, and then her little feet slide to the bathroom. Black, John, and I fell silent. The toilet flushed. The sink ran. The bathroom door opened, and her feet went tipping back to her room. We waited until we heard her door click closed.

"Brother told Black where those dudes hang, over in Brownsville. I know that area. Used to do business over there. I'll handle it," John continued, now almost whispering.

I nodded.

"Oh, and Black's girl . . ." My dad paused.

"Kim." Black helped him out.

"Yeah, Kim. She over at Noodles's and them's house right now, checking on Needles."

"Yeah, man. She's studying up to be an EMT. Wanted to make sure he was all stabilized and whatnot. No concussion and stuff, y'know? Those things can kill you if you ain't careful," Black explained.

"Yeah," I said, even though I was thinking, Concussion?

You can die of a concussion? Now I was panicking at the thought of Needles dying from something that I hadn't known how to do anything about.

"Kim should be over here in a second. I asked for her to come and give us—well, really, give you the rundown on what's happening with him," Black said as compassionate as he could.

Moments later my father was opening the door. It was Kim, all smiles, though she wasn't really smiling. But she kind of was. I got the feeling she was one of those people who was so nice that even when she didn't mean to be smiling, she was. She was carrying a leather shoulder bag like a professor. I could tell it was heavy by the way it was digging into her arm, plus she was leaning a little to the left like she had a crooked spine or a gimp leg or something.

"Hey," she said as she stepped inside.

Black got up and took the bag from her, and gave her a kiss. Then he took her by the hand and led her over to the couch and gave his seat up so that she could sit down. It was all pretty sweet. And corny. Black treated her like she was the flyest girl alive. Kim wasn't bad, but she wasn't as hot as Candace, but obviously Candace wasn't the kind of girl for me. But if I had a girl like Kim, I'd probably be acting like a cornball too. And I'd be cool with that.

"So wassup? What's going on over there?" Black asked while setting Kim's overloaded bag on the floor.

I braced myself for the worst. I just knew that Kim would say that Needles is bleeding to death on the inside, and that he's got something wrong happening in his brain, and that I better rush over there right now if I want to see him one last time.

"Not much. Needles will be fine. His wrist is sprained and bruised pretty bad, but the bone didn't break, thank goodness," Kim said. She looked over at me, grinning. "He had a pretty unique bandage on it—kept it stabilized. I didn't get any sign that any of the bones in his face were broken either, just a lot of bruising. I checked his eyes, and asked him about his stomach, if he felt light-headed or queasy, and he said no. I asked him if he felt dizzy or had headaches at all, and he said no. So I don't think he has a concussion, either. He's just all bruised up. He seems to be a pretty tough kid. But he was lucky to have Ali there to look after him, and make sure he was taken care of."

That made me smile, but I turned my head. Didn't want anyone to think I was a show-off.

"Well, thank God for that," my father said, relief in his voice.

"Was Noodles there?" I asked.

"He's the one who let me in."

"Did he say anything?"

"About what?"

"I don't know, about anything?"

I couldn't help it, it was stupid, I know! But I was worried about Noodles, even though I tried not to be. But I knew, now he was all alone too. The two people who he always knew would put up with his crap had decided to bow out. I mean, it was his own fault, but still. And I wasn't sure what kind of guy Noodles was when he was depressed and alone. I wasn't sure he was the type who could handle it or not. Some people out there feel like when life gets tough, they can't cope, and next thing you know, crazy things happen. My mother said she sees it happen with her clients all the time.

"Yeah, he did when I asked him was everything all right, and if he was going to be able to take care of his brother while his mom was gone. She wasn't there, and I kind of got the sense she was almost never there. What's that about?" But Kim kept on talking, running away from the "Where's their mother?" conversation. "Well, whatever. Anyway, so I asked him that, and he told me yeah. And then he started spilling about how he's really blown it, and that Needles won't speak to him or even look at him. He said every time he goes in the room to check on him, Needles rolls over, even though it obviously hurts like hell to do so. I could tell he was trying to be tough and not cry, and I didn't know what to tell the poor kid, so I just gave him a hug."

I didn't say nothing. I just sort of let the words bounce around inside.

"Oh, and when I was leaving, he apologized to me—to us, Kenny—for how he acted the other day when you were cutting their hair. He seemed genuine about it, so I told him not to worry about it." She looked at Black—Kenny, as she called him—and gave him a sweet grin. "So babe, if you see him, treat him regular. He's forgiven. He's got enough on his plate, and something tells me he's learning his lesson in a much harder way than he ever thought."

Like a phantom, Jazz came popping up from around the corner. I knew she would show up as soon as she heard the voice of a woman who wasn't Doris. She was protective in that way. Or maybe just nosy.

"Who's that?" she asked.

My father looked shocked, as if he didn't see this coming. As if he didn't know there was no way Jazz was going to let the voice of another woman in our house slide, without finding out what was what, and who was who, and what was who doing in our apartment.

"Jazz," he called to her, waving her closer. "This is Kim. Kim is Black's girlfriend."

"Oh. Hi, Kim." Jazz held out her hand. "Nice to meet you."

"Nice to meet you, Jazz," Kim said, flashing that smile.

Jazz looked Kim up and down in a split second.

"Nice shoes."

Kim chuckled. I glanced down at Kim's shoes. They were nice. Hadn't even noticed them.

"Thanks, Jazz. They look a lot better than they feel! These things are killing me!"

"Is it pinching in the toe or rubbing on the heel?"

"Girl. It's—"

"Uh. Excuse me," Black interrupted with perfect timing. "We gotta go." Jazz and Kim both looked at Black, shrinking him down to nothing.

"Anyway, nice meeting you, Jazz."

"You too, Kim," Jazz said, wrapping her arm around John's waist again.

John bent down and kissed her forehead, and told her that he would be right back, that he needed to speak to Black outside for a second.

When they all left, Jazz took her seat on the couch and turned the TV back on. The stupid show seemed to pick up right where it left off. I ran over to the window to watch John and Black, but then caught myself and stepped away a little. Didn't seem like a good idea to be too close to the window, y'know, in plain sight. But I could still see John and Black talking. The thought of my dad planning some sort of hit was crazy, but I knew that's what was happening. John and Black talked a while, both using their hands a lot, which let me know that the conversation was pretty serious. John kept pointing to his car, and Black kept nodding his head in agreement. I kept thinking about that gun I saw. I knew that's what John kept referring to. He was probably letting Black know that he had heat and that there ain't no choice but to drive to Brownsville and off whoever was looking for me. Black started shaking his head no, obviously trying to talk my father out of it. But it didn't seem to be working. Then they shook hands and hugged, my father waved to Kim, and he jogged back toward the door.

The rest of the day went pretty smooth if you didn't count the fact that I knew I was being hunted, which I have to tell you is a pretty jacked-up feeling. Like I said, I steered clear of windows, and kept Jazz away too. John knew that I was stressed about everything, so he made sure that the rest of the night was cool. We both knew we couldn't let Jazz know what was going on, because if I told her that some dudes were looking for me, it would've been the world's first case of a child literally crying themselves to death.

So the three of us watched movies—Jazz's picks, of course—and Jazz and I listened to John tell a bunch of stories about how we were when we were younger. I'd heard most of them a million times, but it was nice to watch Jazz take them all in for the first time. John told her that she was talking way before she was walking, which everyone thought was so strange. Made total sense to me! He said she would crawl around speaking in complete sentences about what she wanted and what she didn't want, but couldn't figure out how to stand up and put one foot in front of the other. John said he would always just say to her, "Little girl, stand up," because he knew she understood him. Then one day he said it, and she just did it! I remember that. He said that's how he and my mother knew that Jazz would be an old soul.

He did tell one story I had never heard before. He said that when I was three or four, I would go to bed every night with a stuffed dog him and Doris got me. I remember the dog's name was Roofus. John said he would come to tuck me in, and I would make sure Roofus was lying flat on my stomach, with the covers over him, too. He said I would be holding and hugging Roofus so tight that after a while the stuffing started coming out of him. Every night my father would do this, and before he'd leave the room, he'd ask two questions. The first was whether or not I wanted the nightlight on. I always said no. The second was whether I wanted the door closed or cracked. I always said closed. John said that one night, when he was tucking me in, he asked the two questions, and I answered like I always answered. Then he said, "You're so lucky. You don't have to be afraid of the dark because you have Roofus here to protect you." I looked at him and laughed, and said, "No, Daddy. Roofus is lucky. I protect him." And now he said that's why he really wasn't surprised about me taking up for Needles, that I've been that way since I was young.

By the time my mother got home, the three of us were knocked out on the couch, John and I slumped side by side, Jazz laid out across our laps. I heard the knob turn and the door open, and by the time I could lift my head, John's head was up too.

"Ma?" I whispered, my throat full of sleep.

"Lord have mercy, look at y'all," she said, touching the top of my head as she walked behind the couch. "Get your little sister up and go to bed."

I slowly slid out from under her legs and scooped her up in my arms like a baby.

"Night, Dad," I whispered to John.

"Good night, Ali."

In my room I lay in bed, lights off, but I left the door cracked for the first time in my life. I tried to go to sleep, but my brain was going in a trillion bad directions, wondering what would happen when the sun came up. When it was daytime again, what terrible thing might go down? Was my father going to really go to kill those guys? Was he really going to put his life in danger for me? Then I started thinking about if I would do that for him. Would I risk getting killed, or at least getting the crap beat out of me? Would I do that for Jazz? For Doris? Of course I would. I did it for Needles!

It was so much to swallow. What if John gets caught? What if he goes back to jail for shooting someone again, but this time for life? What if he misses and they shoot him! Oh, man! What if he can't find them and they find me first? And in that moment, I thought that maybe helping Needles was a mistake. Maybe it was a mistake so big that my father, and my family, would be paying for it forever.

★ 15 ★

I woke up early the next morning. Well, I don't know if you can really call it waking up, since I never actually got to sleep. I rolled out of bed and hurried into the living room to see John, hoping he hadn't already taken off for Brownsville. It was important for me to see him, to talk to him, not that I could talk him out of it. I'm not even exactly sure that I wanted to. But just to see him and talk to him. You just never know, and I didn't want him leaving, and something happening, and me not catching him to say good-bye before he left.

I hadn't heard any arguing or anything like that in the middle of the night, so I assumed it was cool with Doris for him to stay here. When I came into the living room, the two of them were sitting on the couch having coffee. I couldn't believe my eyes. My parents together in the morning. And they actually seemed natural around each other.

"Morning," I said, trying not to make things awkward.

"Morning, Ali," John said.

"Hi, sweetie," Doris said. She stood up, gave me a kiss

on the head, and then went to put her cup in the sink. "I'm gonna be late for work. The A train'll probably be all jacked up as usual." She grabbed her bag. "Y'all behave. Ali, look after your sister, and you still ain't allowed out this house. Understand?"

I knew that was coming. I just nodded my head yes.

"And John," she started. She walked over to him. He stood up, and she wrapped her arms around him tight. She whispered something in his ear, and when she pulled away, she whipped toward the door so fast, I couldn't see her face.

"She okay?" I asked.

"Yeah, she's okay. I told her that I was going to go take care of all this drama today in Brownsville, and of course, that has her all shook up."

"So you really going to do it?"

"Ali, I don't see no other choice. Either I handle them or they handle you."

"Or we could just leave Brooklyn."

"Leave Brooklyn? Boy, this is home. You leave home on your terms, not because someone ran you out. Got that?"

"Got it."

We sat quietly for a second, and then I got a whiff of coffee, and bacon, and cinnamon. I glanced over to the kitchen. No pots. No pans. Stove off.

"Hey! Ma cooked for you?" I asked jealously. Doris never cooks breakfast for us because she leaves so early. If she had cooked breakfast for my father, I was going to be salty.

John looked at me crazy and laughed. "Now, you know

your mother ain't make no breakfast," he said, shaking his head. "I think it's Brenda upstairs. Go ahead up there and ask if you can have some."

I laughed. "Ms. Brenda is cool, but she don't seem like the type to share food."

John hooted. "Got that right!"

About twenty minutes later he'd gotten himself together and was about to leave the house. I asked him why he was leaving so early, and he told me something about how if they hustle like Brother said, then they should be wide-awake and on the block, and that it's best to catch them early before they start looking for me. Jazz was still asleep, which was unlike her, but when I thought about it, maybe she just felt more comfortable knowing that John was in the house. We didn't really talk about too much before he took off, or have any sort of amazing father/son lightbulb moment, but the time we spent, to me, was quality. I told him that I loved him, which wasn't too hard to do. I know for most guys it's pretty tough, but because I'm so affectionate toward Jazz, and I'd watched John be the same way, it seemed like a normal thing to say, especially knowing what he was about to do for me.

I asked if he was going to tell Jazz good-bye, and he said that he'd rather not wake her. He told me to do it for him, and to not worry too much because he would be back. But if there is anything I've learned about parents, it's that they always tell you a positive thing in the middle of a negative situation because they don't want you to trip out. And I appreciate that. He reached down and picked up his Yankees fitted cap, brushed it on his thigh, and slapped it on his head. He hugged me tight, and awkwardly, then pushed me away and gave me a left-handed handshake. Not dap. A handshake. Grown-man style. And he squeezed tight. So I squeezed tight. And then he left.

Like usual, I walked over to the kitchen window to see him leave. There was really nothing to it. John just got into his car and pulled off. I leaned to the side to follow the car as far as I could, but before I knew it, it was gone.

When Jazz got up, we did all the things we normally did. I needed things to be as regular as possible to keep my mind off John, and to keep me from acting weird around Jazz, which would then lead her to asking questions and worrying. So, everything went like usual. She cooked breakfast. I tried to help, but of course she wouldn't let me. Pancakes, eggs, and orange slices. I ate it. We watched her shows. News, talk shows, soap operas. I helped her look through magazines for cool scrapbook pages while she picked my brain. All of her questions were about our folks. She wanted to know why John had spent the night, and if it was because he and Mom were thinking about getting back together. But I didn't really have an answer for her. To be honest, our parents was the one thing I didn't want to talk about. Not right then. Not with the thought of our dad never returning swimming around my head like goldfish in a shark tank. So I talked around all her questions, never really giving her any direct answers. After a while she just stopped asking and zoned back in to the TV.

I took the bowls we used for lunch to the sink, then

popped into the bathroom to pick something out of my teeth. I examined my mouth, as well as the rest of my face. I noticed the swelling was just about all gone, and the bruises were disappearing. The blue under my eye was turning back to brown.

I heard a thump. But I didn't pay it any mind because this is Brooklyn. You hear lots of things. Then I heard a voice. It was coming from the shower wall, which means it was coming from the apartment next door. Needles and Noodles's place.

I sat on the edge of the tub like I used to, like a fisherman sitting on the edge of his boat, waiting for something good to bite the line. I just listened, wondering who was there. I wanted to say something or do something. Maybe tap on the wall—that way if it was Needles, he would know it was me and maybe say something. But I didn't. I couldn't. The bath faucet dripped slowly, ringing as each drip splashed against the drain. I sat staring at the blue tile on the wall, wishing I had some sort of X-ray vision to see through to the other side. See if Needles was still bruised up bad. See if he was bent over, limping, or if his ribs had healed any so he could at least stand up straight. I wanted to make sure he still had his wrist wrapped up tight and that after he left the bathroom, he went right back to bed to rest up.

I also wished I could see Noodles. Just to see if he was okay, is all. When Kim told me that he apologized to her about how he acted at Black's house, I couldn't help but feel bad. Not that he didn't owe her an apology, but if he humbled himself enough to actually say he was sorry, then he must really be flipping on the inside. I mean, both me and his brother had lost faith in him, so everything had to be finally starting to get to him. And even though he had every bit of what he was going through coming to him, he was still my best friend. He was still my homeboy. My road dog. My dude. So I couldn't help but worry, even when I felt like he didn't deserve my worry anymore.

"Ali, you okay?" Jazz's voice snapped me out of my trance. She tapped on the door lightly. "Ali?"

A drop of water hit the drain.

"Yeah, I'm cool, Jazz. Coming out in a second," I said. I tried to put some smile in my voice so that she didn't worry or ask any questions. I could tell that she could sense something, though. That's the only reason she came and knocked on the door. Any other time she would've just assumed that I was using the bathroom, maybe going number two. But this time she came looking for me.

"Stupid orange stuff," I said, opening the door.

"Pulp."

"Yeah, pulp," I said, smirking. "Stuck all in my teeth."

Jazz looked at me and twisted her mouth up. I knew she didn't believe me, but I also knew she knew that whatever I wasn't telling her, I wasn't telling her for a reason.

A few hours later Jazz was taking her usual midday nap, the scandal of soap opera playing in the background, probably providing her with dreams no eleven-year-old should ever have, and I was sitting on the couch just waiting for something to happen. I didn't know what that something was going to be. Maybe a devastating phone call from my mother saying she got word my father was dead, killed by some punks in Brownsville. Or maybe Black would come by and tell me that my father was down at the precinct, arrested for attempted murder or something like that. I don't know, but I knew something was coming, and I was waiting for it.

Somewhere between the television saying "I thought you died in the car crash" and "I love you too much to let you marry him," I heard a key being pushed into the deadbolt. I turned the TV off and sprung up as the knob turned and the door opened.

I didn't know I was holding my breath until I saw him— my dad. Thank God! He stood in the doorway, filling up the space like a broken-down grim reaper. He held the bottom of his shirt up to his nose, using it to plug his left nostril to stop blood from pouring from it. He limped inside, wincing, with a duffel bag hiked up on his shoulder. Jazz twitched, reacting to whatever dream she may have been having. Afraid to wake her and have her freak out, my dad put a finger up to his lips, mouthed, *Be quiet*, and walked lightly to the kitchen sink. I met him there, grabbed the hand towel we dry dishes with, wet it with cold water, and gave it to him. He pressed it against his nose and leaned against the kitchen counter, his head tilted back, his eyes teary. I stood in front of him, staring at him as if he wasn't real. Looking at his hands, thinking that they were now the hands of a murderer. Looking at his nose, wondering which guy hit him before he blew them all away.

As happy as I was to see him here, alive, I'd never, ever,

ever in my whole life felt worse about the fact that he had to do what he did for me. To protect me. Because I had to protect Needles since Noodles wouldn't. But then again, it was me who pressed for Needles to go with us to that stupid party in the first place! Not Noodles. It was me. So it was just as much my fault as anyone's. I just couldn't believe that any of this was happening. Everything had come undone. And I had no idea what to say to my dad, or what he would say to me.

Once he finally got his nose to stop bleeding, he motioned toward my room. We tiptoed down the hall, my knees barely bending, my ankles mushy and loose. I felt like I was going to pass out or something. The hallway seemed longer than usual, and even though it was the middle of the afternoon, it felt like midnight. We slipped in and closed the door, slowly turning the knob to make sure it didn't click and wake up Jazz.

John sighed a long drawn-out sigh, like a heavy load had just come out of him and was now floating around the room. It sort of felt like it came out of his mouth, bounced around the walls for a moment, and then landed right on my shoulder. Or right on top of my head. The heaviness of the room, the tension, the fact that John hadn't said nothing about anything yet, broke me. I threw myself at him just because I was so scared and confused, I didn't know what else to do. He wrapped his arms around me as I sobbed. My shoulders were like bouncing all over the place as I hiccuped and snorted— just ugly. This was the kind of cry that could get you laughed at forever if the wrong dude saw you. Lucky it was my dad, and though I had never really cried in front of him before, he was cool about it. He didn't say stop crying, or toughen up. He just said to let it out.

"It's okay, Ali. It's all over now. I took care of it like I said I would," John said, his voice trembling.

"What you mean?" I snuffed out.

"What you mean, what I mean? I took care of it. You don't gotta worry about nobody coming to get you," he said, his arms pushing me away from him so he could see my face. "You understand? I handled it. Needles and Noodles are safe too. It's over." He spoke like he was sure. Like he did something to permanently prevent them from coming after me. I knew what that something was, but I still had to make sure. There was something about hearing it that made it real, and even though I really didn't want to hear it, I kind of did.

"Can I ask you something?" I said, wiping my face, easing down onto the bed. "What was it like?"

"What was what like?" John asked, still standing, leaning against the wall, Muhammad Ali posed behind him, taped to the wall with a big cheese on his face.

"Pulling the trigger."

"Pulling the . . ." John stopped midsentence. "Wait," he said, walking over to the bed. He sat down beside me and went through a quick series of motions, from glancing at the ceiling, to wiping his face with his hands, to patting my back before continuing, "You think I shot them? You think I went over to Brownsville and killed those dudes, Ali?"

My confusion reached an all-time high.

"Yeah. Ain't that what you did? Took care of it?"

John sat silent for a second.

"Yeah, I took care of it, Ali, but I ain't kill nobody! Why you even think something like that? You ain't never known me to be wild like that, have you?"

"No, but I saw that gun in your car, and I know back in the day, you—"

"I shot a man at a bodega, and you thought I was gonna shoot them fools, too. Right," John said, suddenly piecing it all together. I could tell he felt bad about me thinking that, but it's not like I was just coming from left field with this whole thing.

"Son, I ain't shoot nobody today, and I won't shoot nobody ever again. Trust me. That gun don't even got no bullets in it, and to be honest, my ass can't afford to buy none." John smirked. "I'm sorry you even had to see that."

I straightened up.

"So how you take care of it, then?" I asked.

John stood up and stuck his thumbs in his pockets like he always used to make me do when my mother made me tuck my shirt in. "Slouch your pants down a little, boy. You look crazy with your pants all up on your chest like that," he'd joke.

He resumed his position in front of the poster of the champ. "I went over there, to the corner Brother said they hang on. I pulled right up to them and jumped out the car. It was two of them, and they both looked pretty rough, but the biggest one looked real bad. And by bad, I don't mean mean, I mean bad. Like somebody whooped up on him, bad. So I figured I would just flat-out come at him. I said, 'Yo, man, you know a cat in Bed-Stuy name MoMo,' and he ain't say nothing, probably because he thought I was the feds or something like that. So then I said, 'Yo, I don't want no trouble or nothing, and it ain't even like that.' And then big man was like, 'Why you askin' 'bout MoMo?' which let me know that he did know MoMo and that he was probably one of your victims, Ali. The dude looked horrible. He had some lumps, but the worst part was he had a missing tooth! You really gave that brother the business."

John gave me a proud look and continued, "So then I just came out with it. I just said, 'Look, man, you, or some of your boys, came around Bed-Stuy looking for a kid y'all got in a fight with at MoMo's party Wednesday night." Man, as soon as I said that, they got even more serious, chests all poked out, hands reaching under their shirts, thinking I came to bring the heat. So I told them quickly, again, that it wasn't like that.

"Then one of them was like, 'You know him? You know where he at?' and I was like, yeah. And they told me to tell them and that they would break me off something if I did. One of them flashed some cash, and the other one flashed some coke. Then I told them I was your father."

"And what did they say to that?" I asked, listening to the story like it was one of Noodles's comics. My father just stood there, all cool, telling the story with his thumbs tucked in like a ghetto cowboy. He could have told the story wearing sunglasses, but then none of it would've been believable, even though he definitely was sounding cool enough to pull it off.

"What did they say?" John repeated. "What did they say? Man, they started trippin'. The big one yoked me all up, and before I knew it, the other dude came and popped me in the nose. Then a sucker punch to the gut knocked all the wind out of me. Then they started talking about how I shouldn't be trying to play hero, and that they were gonna find you and handle you, and all that kinda stuff. And that's when I told them that I ain't come for no beef, but that I came to talk. To negotiate."

Negotiate?

"And what you negotiate?" I asked.

John took his thumbs from his pockets and folded his arms.

"Everything, son." His eyes suddenly filled with water. "I negotiated everything. I told them that I had a car full of expensive clothes. At least ten grand worth. And they could have it all. Hell, I even told them they could have the damn car. But I made sure they knew that the catch is, they gotta leave you and your homeboys alone. They agreed, we shook on it, and I grabbed my bag out the passenger seat and dropped the keys in the big guy's hand. They made me wait while they searched the car and checked out all the merchandise. They couldn't believe what they were seeing and what I was offering. One of them mentioned something about how they wish they had a father like me, or whatever. Next thing I knew, they hopped in my car and took off."

My dad's cool was now overflowing and running down the side of his face and neck. I sat on the bed, uncomfortable, weird, unsure of what to say or do. He had sacrificed every-thing for me.

"What you gonna do now?" I asked.

"You know me, Ali. I'll figure something out, man." John forced a half smile and wiped his face with the palm of his hand. I wanted to ask him where he was going to stay, but I didn't want him to know that I knew he lived in his car. I just couldn't say anything that might embarrass him. After what he did for me—no way.

★ 16 ★

I heard my mother's footsteps before I saw her face. It was a little after five, and the door downstairs, the one that lets you into our building, opened, followed by the sound of the fastest feet I've ever heard rushing up the steps. When she opened the door, John, Jazz, and I were all sitting on the couch chitchatting. John turned to her, and even though I couldn't see his face, I knew he gave her a big smile, a stupid funny one, because her eyes instantly bugged out and her hand flew over her mouth as if she wanted to scream, or maybe smile. Or maybe both. But like a parent, she knew not to make a scene. Not with Jazz right there. So she quickly shook off her shock and tried to act normal.

"Turn that damn TV down! What's wrong with y'all?" she snapped, stepping over John and kissing Jazz and me on the head. "Um, John, can I see you for a second?" she asked as she continued on to the bedroom, dropping her bag at the beginning of the hallway.

"Uh-oh," Jazz said, teasing. "You in trouble. I ain't even

know the TV was that loud." Jazz shook her head like an old lady as my father headed to the bedroom. Judging from my mother's reaction when she came in the door, I figured that John must have told her the same thing he told me, which was that he was going to go "handle it." So my mother, I suspected, thought the same thing I did, that history was going to repeat itself, and John was going to shoot somebody and wind up in jail. Again. Or maybe worse—dead. So the fact that he made it home alive made her happy but also worried her because she knew, or at least she thought she knew, what he had done. After about twenty-five minutes my parents came from the room, my mother patting a tissue against her eyes, my father's hand on her back. She picked her bag back up and got ready to head to her second job, but before she left, she made me and Jazz stand up to hug her. She hugged us for a crazy long time.

"Will you be here when I get back?" she asked John, who was leaning on the kitchen counter, watching.

"I'll be here," he said, his voice deep, low, honest.

The next day, Saturday, might have been one of the best days of my life, and the funniest part about it is, nothing really happened. At least nothing superwild, like Doris winning the Mega Millions lottery. Nothing like that. It was actually a pretty simple day, but still one of the best I've ever had, and I bet Jazz would say the same thing. We—all of us—got up around nine. I got to watch Doris call in to her job and pretend to be sick, which is something she never did. She put on some fake scratchy "I'm about to die" voice, while John and I made funny faces and joked her. She finished the call from her bedroom to keep from laughing. Plus, she didn't want Jazz to see her lying, even though something told me that Jazz already knew about calling out sick, and how most people aren't really sick.

Then John and I cooked the ladies breakfast. Pancakes, eggs, sausage, and orange juice. John insisted that I learn his pancake technique. By the way, he still calls pancakes "flap-jacks," which is hilarious. He's got a whole thing when it comes to flipping them. He counts to eighty-seven, and then he flips the pancake by tossing it in the pan. He said eighty-seven seconds got them to be perfect golden brown, and I must admit, most of them were perfect. The only thing is, most of them also ended up on the floor, on the counter, in the sink, everywhere but back in the pan. After a while he got frustrated and a little embarrassed, and just started using a spatula like everyone else. Jazz and Doris nearly passed out from laughing so hard, but as the chef's assistant, I did my best to keep a straight face.

The rest of the day we all just loafed around, talking trash and flipping through page after page of Jazz's scrapbook. Even Doris looked at them. It was cool to see all the images Jazz had created, from Mom and Dad standing on top of a whale in the middle of the ocean, to all of us standing in front of the pyramids in Egypt.

"What's this one?" Doris asked, studying a page that looked way different from the rest.

Jazz leaned over. "Oh, that's you and Dad on the moon."

Mom smiled and yelped, "The moon?" and held the book up so we all could get a better look. It definitely was a strange picture. You couldn't really tell it was Doris and John at all. It just looked like four arms and four legs, connected to one big astronaut helmet. Doris continued, "Well, why do we look like that?"

I almost snotted trying to hold in a laugh.

Jazz rolled her eyes at me and explained, "See, when I was making this one, I realized that y'all wouldn't be able to breathe on the moon. So I needed to find pictures of astronaut helmets to give you. But I could only find one. So I had to make y'all share it." Jazz examined the page. "Didn't come out perfect, but—"

"Yes, it did, sweetie," Doris said, nodding. "It's perfect. The only thing is, your daddy got a big ol' head, so I don't know if mine could really squeeze in there with his."

We all laughed, except John, who reached over and turned to the next page.

Later my mother surprised all of us by announcing that she was cooking dinner. Though we had already spent most of the day snacking, it was still a pretty awesome announcement, and we all were shocked by it. It's not that she couldn't cook. As a matter of fact, she could whip up some of the best food anybody on earth ever had, with any kind of meat, a can of chicken broth, a head of lettuce, some olive oil, and some Season-All. But she was out of practice. She never cooked. She was always working, and when she wasn't, Sundays, she was too busy resting to worry about making us food. That's why she taught Jazz how to cook so young. But on this day, a Saturday, a "sick day," she decided that she would cook dinner, but she wouldn't tell us what she was going to make. We all took guesses, but she wouldn't crack. She wanted it to be a surprise.

Me, Jazz, and John sat outside on the stoop, while my mother walked around the corner to the store to buy whatever she needed for the special dinner. The sun was coming down and had just tucked itself behind the brownstones. It was a beautiful Brooklyn summer evening, the hydrant spraying water all over everything, the sidewalk, the cars, the kids. All the little girls, hair dripping, poofed up and frizzy. The boys were soaked, their jean shorts now baggier than normal. The ice-cream truck was parked in the middle of the block, engine off, annoying song chiming over and over again, as babies jumped off the bottom step of their stoops and ran over with their change to bargain for a Rocket Pop.

It was so hot that it seemed like the air was sweating. But it was still a perfect time to be outside. It was like watching our neighborhood tick for the first time. It's funny, I think that may have been Jazz's first time ever sitting on the stoop with me. And I know for sure it was our father's first time sitting on the stoop with us. Doesn't seem like it would be a big deal, but I know that to all three of us it was the biggest deal ever.

A door slammed.

I turned to my left, and there was Noodles standing at the top of his stoop. He squinted and put his hand up to his forehead like an army salute, to block the sun. He looked out onto our block, the kids, the elders, the craziness and the strange calm of it all. He glanced over at me and noticed Jazz and our dad sitting one step down. He looked at us with a weird expression on his face, but it wasn't the usual "I hate my life and I wish I was you" look. This time it was more of a look of embarrassment. Like we had caught him stealing.

We caught eyes as he struggled to get one of his folded-up comics out of his pocket. I wasn't necessarily angry anymore, and honestly, I admit that I was actually kinda glad to see him, even though it was mad awkward. I just didn't know what to say to him. It had been a few days since everything went down, and when you're used to hanging out with a person every single day, a few days off can sometimes seem more like a few months. It felt like in those two or three days I had changed, or at least part of me had changed, somehow. Like, I knew more than I had before, in a lot of ways. All I could do was hope the same was happening to him. But there was no way to tell, and I wasn't really in the mood to talk about none of it. I was having the best day ever and wasn't in the mood for no drama.

But my dad, as cool as he can be, is still a dad. And he does what dads do.

"Roland?" John said. It cracked me up when people called Noodles by his government name. John didn't even call him that normally, but that day he decided to. Maybe it was some sort of, like, symbolic thing he was trying to do. Maybe he was making the point that he was talking to him as John the adult, an elder, not as a friend or coolish kind-of-father dude.

"How you doing, son?" he continued.

Noodles took a seat on the step, second to the top. Needles's seat.

"Fine," he said softly.

"Good, good."

Thick silence.

A door opened, this time behind me.

"Look at y'all, looking like a perfect scene from a Spike Lee movie." It was Ms. Brenda, dressed all up in her Saturday's best, which was the same as her Friday's best, except on Saturday she wore sandals with a heel. Fridays, no heel. Oh, and Saturdays was always red lipstick day, and for some reason that kinda made sense to me.

"Hi, Ms. Brenda!" Jazz said, excited to see her.

"Jazmine, honey, how are you?" Ms. Brenda asked. She was always so sweet.

"Fine," Jazz said.

"You looking after these three boys?"

"Yes," Jazz said, her face all proud.

"Good, 'cause Lord knows they need it!" Ms. Brenda laughed.

My dad laughed too.

"Come on, Brenda, we ain't that bad, are we?"

Ms. Brenda looked at him like he had a third eye and a third lip.

"Dang. You tough!"

Ms. Brenda smiled, chuckling to herself, while squeezing past us.

The sun was sinking down a little more, and the street-lights started to buzz and fade in. I guess my father could sense the tension between Noodles and me. We all could probably feel it. So, John did what parents do—he minded my business. Which normally would've pissed me off, but how could I really be mad after he "minded my business" the day before?

"Come here, Roland," he said, stretching to see over the stone stoop banister. Noodles sat slumped like a defeated king on a broken throne. When my father called him, he slowly stood. I didn't look over at him, but I could tell he was moving slowly. I was focused on the back of my father's head. I was probably trying to see if I could get a glimpse of what in the world was on his mind, even though I already knew. He was about to try to play Mr. Fix-a-Friendship, which I wasn't really down with. I just felt like maybe it would fix itself over time, and that there was no need for my father to stick his nose in it.

I caught Noodles in the corner of my eye as he sort of limped down the steps.

"Sit down," my father demanded, bumping Jazz over to make more space beside him on the step.

Noodles eased down onto the concrete slab.

"How's he doing, your brother?"

"He's okay. Better."

"Did you do everything Kim said? Keep his bandages clean and all that stuff? She wrote you a list, right?"

"Yeah, I stuck to it."

"Good."

Noodles glanced up at me. I looked down at him.

Thick silence, again.

A few minutes later my mother came bopping down the street, trying her best to steer a shopping cart with a wobbly wheel. My father looked at her with squinted eyes, then shook his head.

"That's Ma?" Jazz said, standing up to get a better look.

"Yeah, that's her."

My mother pushed the cart like she was walking a big dog, a Rottweiler. She was all over the sidewalk, swerving and yanking every which way, the plastic bag handles flapping in the wind like white flags. It was quite a scene.

"Hey, y'all," she said, out of breath. "I had too much stuff to try to carry it all home, so Manu, you know, Manu who be outside straightening up the carts? He told me to just take one and bring it back."

Then my mother looked at Noodles.

"Hey, Noodles." She smiled.

"Hi, Ms. Doris."

"How you, son?"

"Fine."

My mother looked at my father and communicated something to him without speaking. Some secret ESP parent thing. Then she turned back to Noodles. "Good. Come up for some dinner later, if you want. I'll make your brother a plate too," she added, stepping past him and patting him on the head. The pat was harder than a "cute little kid" pat. It was more jokey. More of a "You better come to dinner" type of thing, which I definitely wasn't expecting. It was like my parents had turned on me.

Noodles managed a little smile and scooted over to let her pass. When she got to the door, she asked John to bring the bags up, and told Jazz to help.

"And Ali, you and Noodles take that cart back around to the store. I told Manu I would bring it right back." Doris smirked and turned toward the door. Just before she went in, she turned back around. "By the way, it's barbecue chicken tonight."

John literally jumped up in the air, he was so happy. I was pretty happy too. It was my favorite, and I had no idea until right then that it was his favorite too.

I pushed the wobbly cart up the block. By now it was dark, and the streetlights were like spotlights highlighting fire hydrants, and kids out after curfew. Noodles walked a few feet away from me. I could tell he didn't want to be doing this, but no way was he saying no to Doris. We didn't say nothing to each other until we got to the top of the block, and we waited for the light to change.

"Stupid wheel," I said, giving the cart a shake. I had to say something.

"Yeah, Manu should go ahead and trash this one," Noodles agreed.

"Right."

The light changed.

We headed for the supermarket and didn't say another word to each other until we started walking back.

"So, Needles is good?"

"Huh?"

"You told my dad Needles is good. Is he?" I asked, trying to sound somewhere in the middle.

"Yeah, he's good," Noodles said, shoving his hands in his pockets. "It's just, y'know, tough."

I played dumb, mainly because I knew he wanted to talk about it. I wanted to talk about it too. "What's tough?"

"Everything. I mean, he won't even talk to me. Won't even look at me if he can help it. I really did it this time, Ali. You mad at me, he mad at me, I'm mad at me." He ripped a fistful of leaves off a scraggly tree we were walking by. "Man, I don't know what to do."

"Yeah," I said, preparing myself for what I was about to say, because I had decided right then and there to swallow my pride. "But I gotta apologize to you too, for my part in all this mess. I pushed for him going to the stupid party in the first place. You didn't want him to go. I did."

"Yeah, but he should've been able to go anyway. I mean, he ain't really no different from us. He just got a syndrome, but man, the way I been feeling, and when I think about the way I act sometimes, shoot, I probably got some kind of syndrome too."

A laugh snorted out of me. "Me too!"

"And I know this wrong, man, but the way you hit them fools the other night, they probably got a couple syndromes too now!"

We both snort-laughed, and then Noodles's laughter drifted off.

"Speaking of all that, I heard they looking for us." Noodles's voice went from joking to real worried, in a snap.

"My dad took care of all that. Nothing to trip about."

"Dad? You mean John?" He nodded, almost to himself. "Hey, that's cool. But what about me and Needles?"

"He took care of it for y'all, too. We all together in this."

Noodles didn't say nothing.

"Nood, I gotta ask you something. Did you apologize to your brother yet?" That question had been rattling around my mind for a while now, because even though I hoped that Noodles had made some changes, I wasn't so sure that he had come square with Needles.

"Yeah, man, but he ain't say nothing. I don't think he believes me." Noodles started folding up those pitiful leaves like he folded up his comic book pages. Clearly, he had a syndrome too—a folding syndrome.

We were waiting for the light to change again.

"Honestly, he probably don't. Gotta show him. Not trying to be soft, but that's the way things go. Shoot, man, I been learning that a lot lately over at my place."

The light changed.

Once we got back to my stoop, we sat at the top, side by side, and watched nothing and everything. The smell of barbecue sauce was seeping from the window upstairs, seducing the whole hood. Ms. Brenda was walking up the block, stopping every few steps to chat with someone else. Black had his cab at the end of the block and was looking under the hood. Kim was in the driver's seat, starting the car every time he gave her the signal. The radio was up loud, but it wasn't no music coming out of the speakers. Instead it was some mess about medical stuff. Like a book on tape or something. Must've been Kim's, but when it comes to Black, you just never know. It might've been his. Old man Malloy was being wheeled down the sidewalk by little Joe. Malloy glanced over at me, at us, and just nodded his head. I don't know what that meant exactly, but I took it as something good.

Then all of a sudden, out of the blue, Noodles decided to break down how, over the last few days, with all the time to himself, he figured out why he loved comics so much. He was holding those folded leaves like they were pages from his actual comics.

"It's because the main dude is always like some guy who really wants to do good but always messes up. He's like . . . like . . ." Noodles couldn't find the word.

"Misunderstood?"

"Yeah! They always misunderstood."

"Uh-huh. So now you think you Incredible Hulk, huh?"

"Naw, you saw me the other night. I'm Mr. Invisible!"

We both laughed, and just like that, we were cool again. Noodles continued to dissect all the stuff he thought was deep about comics, and how when he draws them, he adds tattoos and jewelry and stuff like that to make them more current. I was just listening and trying not to clown him, and even told him that I still had the one he gave me when we first met, when all of a sudden a door slammed.

Noodles and I both jumped up and looked over at their

apartment, thinking that maybe it was Needles coming out to join us. But it wasn't. Actually, it was his mother, Ms. Janice, dressed in a mini skirt and a mini-er shirt, trotting down the steps, holding an overnight bag.

"Hi, Ms. Janice," I said, to be respectful.

"Hi, baby," she said, like it was a reflex to respond that way.

Noodles just sat back down on the stoop, flicking those folded leaves down the steps.

As usual, a car pulled up. This time a Benz the color of wet sidewalk. Ms. Janice pulled her skirt down as she slipped into the car, everyone on the block watching her. I purposely didn't look at Noodles. I could tell he was uncomfortable, and it instantly reminded me of the first day I met him on that stoop, and how embarrassed he was that he lived in a slum house, a place everybody knew junkies and hookers hung out at. Most of our neighbors still felt that way about that house, and I think now the reason why is mainly because of Ms. Janice. And even though I thought it was messed up that his mother didn't say nothing to him when she was leaving, I think, in a weird way, Noodles was cool with it. I don't think he wanted her to.

A few moments after the car pulled off, we heard another door open. Well, the same door as before. Just again. We jumped up, waiting to see who was coming out. We heard grunting, and slow feet dragging, until finally Needles stepped out. He looked good in the sense that he was standing up and walking on his own, but he looked bad in the sense that he just seemed wiped out. He looked like he hadn't slept in days. His face was kinda gray, his lips cracked and rough.

He stood at the top of the stoop and stared out into the busy street, but not at anything or anyone in particular. He didn't even notice me and Noodles sitting on my stoop next door. One of Needles's eyes twitched slightly. It was like he was possessed or in some kind of trance. He stood there like an exhausted climber who had just made it to the peak of a mountain. He wobbled like he could pass out at any given moment.

"Needles!" I shouted, jumping to my feet and charging down the steps in front of my house.

"Needles!" Noodles repeated, following behind me.

All I could think about was that I didn't want Needles to fall. I wouldn't be able to deal with the sight of him tumbling down the concrete stoop.

I was just going to take him by the hand and help him down. But before we could start up the steps toward him, Needles began to scream.

Oh, damn. Damn! He was making a sound that I had never heard before. I don't even really know how to describe it. Maybe like a police siren, and a baby cry, and screeching tires all mixed up. He held it as long as he could, and when he ran out of breath, he did it again. In between screams he would shout a cuss word or something strange, but then he'd go right back to the screaming.

Everyone—the whole block—froze. The kids stopped

splashing in the hydrant, stuck, not sure if they should laugh or cry. Little Joe stopped pushing his grandfather, Malloy, who snatched his sunglasses from his face. Kim turned the radio down in the car, and Black popped his head out from under the hood. And me and Noodles stood there, like our feet were melting into the concrete. We didn't know what to do.

Kim began to run toward us. Black chased behind her, yelling for her to stay away just in case Needles was dangerous. But Kim said she knew he wouldn't hurt her. They started up the steps, and the closer they got, the more Needles stepped back.

"We're not gonna hurt you, Needles," Kim said in her usual sweet way, but Needles kept screaming, now pressed against that door, screaming, screaming.

Kim and Black backed down a few steps, confused.

"I don't know what to do. It's like he's scared of us," Kim said, her face pale.

"This happened before," I told her, my brain finally working again.

"Knitting stuff!" Noodles cried. "I'll go ask your mom— maybe she got some more." He ran into my building, almost knocking my dad over as he was racing out.

"What is that?" John asked, gaping at Needles.

"He's having some kind of meltdown!" I told him.

Another thing I learned that day is that parents always have more than one of everything. Even random stuff like yarn and knitting needles. Just like that, my mother came flying out the front door, another ball or roll or whatever you call it of yarn in her hand and two more needles. Noodles came running out behind her.

By now, everybody was in on it. Ms. Brenda stood on the third step speaking sweet things to Needles, but I'm sure he couldn't even hear her over his own screams. And Malloy, well, being Malloy, he just sat at the bottom of the stoop yelling his head off too. He was hollering at Needles, telling him to relax while he got more and more worked up himself. I didn't see how yelling at someone to calm down would actually get them to calm down. Shoot, if my mother didn't come back out there, Malloy probably would've resorted to his old faithful and offered Needles a drink.

Once Doris started up the stoop, Needles stopped yelling. He watched her warily as she slowly stepped closer, the yarn and needles in her hand. This time the yarn was pink. Once she got all the way up, she held out the yarn like an offering. He looked at her, twitching, tears running down his cheeks.

"Ms . . . Ms. Doris," he stuttered.

My mother got closer to him. Needles said something to her, but he was talking so low, we couldn't hear. My mother nodded and leaned in even closer. Jazz was peeking out from behind my father, who was standing on the first step, ready to protect my mom just in case something went down. I told him that it was okay—that Needles wasn't violent. But something was definitely wrong.

A few moments later my mother calmly turned around and started back down the steps, still holding the yarn. She looked from me to Noodles. Needles started shouting again from the top.

She cleared her throat. "He said . . ." She got choked up and tried again. "He said . . . it hurts. It hurts him, son." She stared down Noodles, frowning. "That's all he said. It hurts." And then she held the yarn and the needles out in front of Noodles, who looked at them the same way he glared at my hand the first day we met, like he wasn't sure.

It hurts. I could tell almost everyone else around us assumed that he meant his injuries. Like Malloy said, the streets had been talking, and the whole block knew, or at least thought they knew, about Needles being beaten up. But me and Noodles knew what he really meant, what this was really about, and now it was Noodles's turn to earn his brother back.

Noodles took the pink yarn and the needles like taking a baton in a relay race, and started up the steps, two at a time. Now tears were leaking from his eyes. For the first time since I had known him, he didn't try to be tough or hard. He didn't even wipe them away.

Everybody moved away from the stoop and drifted back onto the sidewalk.

Needles was pressed flat against the door as Noodles reached the top and extended his hand, offering the yarn and needles to his brother. Needles swore and cursed, saliva building in the corners of his mouth, tears raining down his face, but his eyes were fixed on his brother. Noodles said something, but we couldn't make it out.

Then he said it again.

Then again, but louder, still holding the yarn and needles out in front of him.

"I'm sorry."

Needles's arms went twitching every which way, and he dropped about seventeen F-bombs in a row. But Noodles stayed right there, right up there with Needles, and said it again, matching every F-bomb with "I'm sorry!" Then he repeated, "I'm sorry! I'm sorry, man!" Noodles now screamed, begged, cried out, "Please forgive me!"

The twitch in Needles's arms started to die down.

Noodles continued, "I'm so, so, sorry," his words turning into a mess of tears and whimpers. He stood all hunched over in front of his brother, holding yarn and needles, his whole body heaving.

Needles, on the other hand, had gone totally still. Silent. The twitching had stopped. The screaming was done. And he was no longer cursing. It was like a weird calm had suddenly come over him. He just stood there in front of his bawling brother, face-to-face.

Then he reached out for the yarn.

I wish I could tell you that after all that, everything was like a sweet "happily ever after." But that ain't how life goes. First of all, we never had barbecue chicken that night. Because of all the ruckus outside, Doris forgot all about it and damn near burned the whole house down. But she made up for it by letting my dad stay with us until he gets back on his feet. And he's trying. Hard. Can you believe he's even gonna try working in the stockroom at the store she works at? He's defi-nitely not too hype about nine-to-fiving, and Doris knows better than to quit her day job, but at least they're giving it a shot, which me and Jazz are both superhappy about.

Needles and Noodles are better now. Not perfect, but what is? Needles still sits on the stoop freestyling and knitting his heart out. He tried to teach Noodles how to knit—thought it'd be good for him—but as soon as Noodles realized how hard it was, he quit and said knitting was only for chicks and sissies. Right. But he did draw a picture of a new superhero—his own original character called Knit Man, which Needles and I both thought was corny, but we told Noodles it was cool. Knitting as a superpower—ridiculous!

And whenever I'm not laughing at those fools, I'm boxing. I've even had some real matches! Like in a ring. Against other people! I get crushed most of the time, but I have won a few. One thing's for sure, it's different when you're boxing some-one who also knows how. But whenever I get beat, I just think about that night at the party. That night when I did my thing. And that definitely keeps me going. Doris and Jazz never come to my fights because they're scared to see me get punched in the face. I can understand that, and it's cool. But John and my boys are always there, screaming in the crowd.

A Reading Group Guide for

WHEN I WAS THE GREATEST
by Jason Reynolds

DISCUSSION QUESTIONS

1. In the opening chapter, how does Ali feel about family? How do you know?

2. What are the ages of Needles and Noodles? Which brother acts the oldest? What is ironic about their relationship?

3. Where is the novel set? Why does the author go into such great detail when introducing the setting? How does the setting contribute to the tone?

4. Who is Ali? Discuss his character through his mannerisms, humor, social interaction, interests, and skills? What type of characterization does the author use to introduce Ali to readers?

5. Why do so many characters in the novel have nicknames?

Discuss how Ali, Needles, and Noodles get their nicknames. What effect does this have on each of the characters?

6. How does Noodles treat Needles? How is his treatment of Needles different from the way the neighborhood treats him?

7. How does the author's choice to include the story about the big guy sitting down to knit with the ladies in *KnitWit* make knitting seem more appropriate for Noodles? What was the author's purpose of including this detail?

8. How does Ali know that Noodles is not really a tough dude?

9. What happened to Ali's father? Where is he now? How does Ali feel towards his father?

10. Who is Malloy? How does Malloy feel about fighting? Would Malloy still have trained Ali if Ali said he was mad at his father?

11. What is the relationship between Noodles and Needles and their mother? What type of person is she? What inferences can be made about her character?

12. Who stood up for Noodles to go to the party? Why does this person want Noodles to attend the party?

13. What is the significance of the barbershop incident? How

does the relationship between Ali and Noodles start to change after this incident?

14. What is Brother's point of view of society? How does Brother's character affect the reader's perception of Bed-Stuy? How does Brother's character add to the conflict within the setting?

15. What is the overall impact the author's word choice has on the novel? How does the word choice affect the tone? What is the tone of novel?

16. How does Noodles react when he is under pressure? Does his behavior influence Ali's character?

17. How sympathetic is Ali towards Noodles when they get back from the party? How do you feel towards Noodles?

18. In Chapter 10, we find out why Noodles is really mad at Needles. Do you think he has a valid reason to be mad at him? Does this realization help develop a major theme throughout the novel?

19. How is the conflict in the novel resolved? Was the resolution predictable?

Turn the page for a look at another novel from Jason Reynolds:

THE BOY IN THE BLACK SUIT

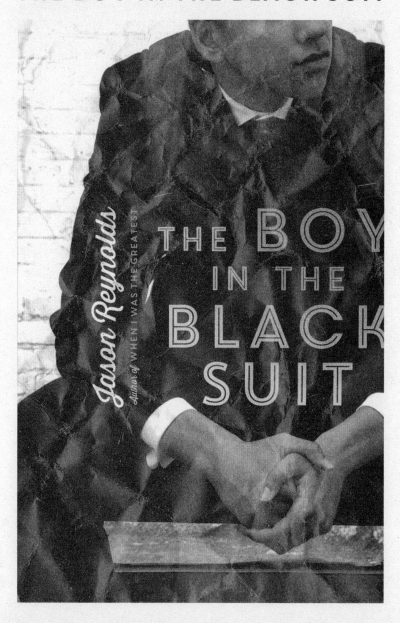

IT WAS THE FIRST DAY OF SCHOOL. ACTUALLY, IT WAS THE nineteenth day of school, but it was *my* first day, and all I could think about was how happy I was that I had already missed three weeks, and that this would be the last first day in this place I would ever have. Thank God. Don't get me wrong, I didn't hate school. I just wasn't really in the mood to be lugging books around, or learning stuff that didn't really matter to me, or even worse, being around people that I didn't really matter to. I know, I know— I sound like a prime candidate for black fingernails and emo poetry, but I guess what I'm really trying to say is that I just wasn't feeling too social. Scratch that—I wasn't feeling social at all. Lockers slamming, sneakers screeching and squeaking on the floor as every kind of teenager ran through the hallways laughing and shouting on their way to class—it was all like one big nail on an even bigger chalkboard. Everyone was zipping by, bumping me, as I sort of floated through the halls like some kind of zombie.

It was like I was living in a different world where everything was backward. Ms. Harris, the principal who normally spent most of her time hiding from students in her office, offered to actually *walk* me to my locker. Meanwhile, kids I was cool with—at least I thought I was cool with—like James Skinner, totally ignored me. See what I mean? Backward.

The last time I saw James was during the summer when our whole class had to meet up at the school to have our senior pictures taken. Me and James joked about how much we hated taking photos, and how our crazy moms were obsessed about the whole thing. I told him how my mother begged me to smile, but I knew I wouldn't. I couldn't. Not because I didn't want to, it's just that every time a camera was pointed at me, I never knew what to do with my face. Some people can smile on cue. You say "smile," and they go ear to ear, flashing every tooth in their mouth. And some people . . . can't. I was one of those. So, I knew in my senior pictures I would look just like I did in my junior, sophomore, and freshman pictures—like a robot. Except this time, it would be a robot face in a cap and gown, which is even worse.

The point is, I had just seen my so-called friend James—had just joked about this corny senior picture crap with him—and now he was acting like he didn't even know me. I guess that's what happens when people find out your mom just died. You become invisible. At least I did. To everybody. Well, almost everybody.

"Yo, Matt, I'm so sorry about your moms, man." Chris Hayes,

my best friend, slid up behind me while I tried to stuff myself into my locker. He was one of those guys who was supercool, crazy fly, and girls had a thing for his shaved head. He'd probably be voted "Best Dressed" or something dumb like that, and if he wanted to, he'd have a fair shot at prom king. And to top it all off, he was trying hard to be sympathetic to me, his pretty normal, now really sad homeboy. I appreciated it even though it did no good. But at least he had enough heart to come up to me and say something, instead of just avoiding me, like death was some kind of disease that anyone could catch just by speaking to me. Everybody else was either staring at me or trying way too hard to not look at me at all.

"Y'know . . . Mrs. Miller was like a second mom to me, and I'm so, so sorry I couldn't make the funeral," Chris went on.

Well, I'm sorry you couldn't make it either. I'm sorry I had to sit there in that church—which, by the way, had a broken air conditioner—sweating, watching all those people march down the aisle to look in my mother's casket and whisper to themselves all this mess about how much she looked like herself, even though she didn't. I'm sorry you weren't there to hear the lame choir drag out, song after song. I'm sorry you weren't there to see my dad try his best to be upbeat, cracking bad jokes in his speech, choking on his words. I'm sorry you weren't there to watch me totally lose it and explode into tears. I'm sorry you weren't there for me, but it doesn't matter, because even if you were, you wouldn't be able to feel what I feel. Nobody can. Even the preacher said so.

That's what I *wanted* to say, but I didn't because Chris didn't deserve all that. I knew he would've been there if he could've. But he just couldn't do it. I get that. So I turned around to look at him and said, "It's all good, man." I swallowed hard and reached out for a five, holding back my tears. *Do. not. cry. Not in school.*

Chris grabbed my hand and pulled me close for a man-hug. And right at that moment, with perfect high-school timing, Shawn Bowman ran up behind Chris, slapped him on the ass, and rambled off some dumb joke, calling us gay or whatever. And of course, after Shawn said that, the girl he was with—Michelle something—smacked him on the arm and sucked her teeth. She yanked Shawn close and whispered in his ear, and I could tell she told him my mom had just died because his face went from blue-black to—well, it stayed blue-black, but if he could've turned red he would've been a walking stop sign. Chris had turned around and glared at Shawn. He had his fists balled up and I could tell he was pissed.

"Asshole," Chris growled. Shawn just slinked away, embarrassed, which, judging by Chris's tone, was a good idea.

It was like all of sudden high school became . . . high school. A bunch of immature, irresponsible teens who felt invincible only because they'd never really been through nothing. The ones who had didn't act like everybody else. Like Shante Jansen. When she got pregnant our sophomore year, she changed big-time. That baby grew her up, and certain things about high school suddenly seemed a lot less important. She just wanted to do her work and go home. No time for the extra silliness. That's how I felt. Like all of a sudden I was way too old for high school, even though I really wasn't. Such a strange feeling.

Luckily, I didn't have to be in school too long. Because I had done pretty good my freshman, sophomore, and junior years, I had a short schedule and could leave at noon everyday. Of course, I was a little behind, but Ms. Harris had all the teachers create make-up assignments for me so that I could catch up on the work I missed. I wasn't really worried too much though. School was always pretty easy for me. A lot easier than smiling, that's for sure.

The original plan was to go to school from eight forty-five to noon, then work at the bank from one to five thirty, as a part of the work-study program. I wasn't too gassed about working at a bank, just because it seemed like it would be boring as hell, sitting behind that thick glass counting other people's money all day. The paycheck, however, I was definitely excited about. But because I missed the first few weeks of school, I also missed the first few weeks of work, and the bank filled my spot with another student. So I was left without a job and nothing to do after class.

My father and I talked when I got word that my spot was being given away, and he told me not to worry about it, but that I should definitely try to find some work, especially since I was going to have so much time on my hands. When he said that, my mother hadn't passed yet. Now that she had, I *really* wanted to find a job, not just to keep busy, but also to try to help him out with the bills. And even though I considered myself to be pretty smart, I didn't have any work experience, at least not any that was on the books. Sweeping Ms. Jones's steps didn't really count.

So I did what anybody in my position would do. I tried to get a job at a fast-food joint. Cluck Bucket. The grimiest spot in the hood. But they were known for paying pretty good. At least more than most of the other fast-food spots. Everybody said it was because it was owned by some rich dude who felt like the least he could do was pay folks enough to survive, since he was practically killing the whole hood with the food. How could something that tastes so good be so bad for you?

I had eaten there tons of times. My mother would send me out to get chicken baskets on Friday nights. We cooked Monday through Thursday and then took the weekend off. Yes, *we* cooked. I was pretty much my mom's sous chef growing up, which is just a fancy way of saying I was her kitchen assistant. A little slicing, a little dicing. Some stirring, some sprinkling. What I'm getting at is, I'm kind of mean with the pot and pan. That's another reason why Cluck Bucket seemed like an easy choice for me. I can burn, and I like the food. Especially the biscuits. My mom always said they reminded her of real country biscuits. I never had a country biscuit, but Cluck Bucket's were incredible. As a matter of fact, Cluck Bucket's everything was pretty good, all the way down to the sweet tea.

"Can I help whoever's next in line?" the girl behind the register said with about as much enthusiasm as I had for anything right now—none. She wore a net on her head that made her hair look more like some kind of helmet, and a gold necklace was around her neck with a nameplate hanging from it. RENEE, it said in cursive.

I stepped forward, my sneakers making that weird sound you hear when something comes unstuck.

"Welcome to Cluck Bucket, would you like to try a combo, a special, the Cluck Deluxe, a shake, or a delicious treat from our list of desserts?" she rattled off while rolling her eyes and looking away.

"Are y'all hiring?" I asked, sort of quietly. I didn't care if anybody knew I was trying to get a job, but at the same time, I didn't want everybody in my business.

Renee looked at me for a second, sizing me up.

"Hold on," she said, annoyed. She turned around and yelled to the back, but it looked like she was yelling at the chicken stacked up in that big metal bed thing it sits in. "Clara. We hiring?"

Another woman appeared from behind the metal trays. Her shirt was white instead of purple like Renee's. She also had that hair thing around her head, but her hair was in braids and looked like snakes caught in a net.

"You looking for a job?" Clara said roughly.

"Yes."

She reached under the register and pulled out a piece of paper. An application.

"Fill this out over there." She pointed toward the tables closer to the door. "And bring it back up here when you done."

Clara then slapped a pen down on the counter and glared at me. "And don't steal my pen."

I sat down and started filling out the application, trying to block out the stale smell of old grease and the sounds of all the people coming in and out, yelling and cracking jokes, kids skipping school, construction workers on their lunch breaks, junkies begging for biscuits, and just about anybody else you could possibly imagine. The bell on the door kept jingling every time someone opened it, letting in the car horns and police sirens from outside. Noise from every damn where.

"What's good, Ma?" a young guy probably my age said to Renee. "You looking good with that thing on your head," he joked. His boys laughed.

I tried to see her reaction, but I couldn't because he was standing in front of her. But I could hear her.

"Yeah, whatever. What you want, man?"

The guy rocked left to right and adjusted the hat on his head, and his crotch.

"What's good with your number?" he said, slick.

"Nope. But how about some food," Renee said pretty flat. I'm sure she got this kind of crap all the time. Some fool crackin' slick in front of his friends. I always wondered if this kind of game worked. Like, does "What's good with your number" really bag the ladies? Doubt it.

"A'ight, a'ight, a'ight, whatever. Just let me get a Deluxe."

"No Deluxes. All out."

"Damn, a'ight. Well, let me get Five Cluck Strips."

"No strips."

"Come on, really?"

"Really."

"A'ight well, just give me a three-piece meal. I *know* you got chicken." The guy laughed and shook his head, disappointed.

At this point he moved to the side, just enough for me to see Renee. She turned around and looked at all the chicken in the hot bed. There must've been like sixty pieces in there. Then she turned back around to the dude.

"All out."

"What?"

"All out. No more chicken."

"It's chicken right there! What you talkin' about?"

"All out."

The boy stood there stunned.

Renee smirked and lifted her hands to her face, her fingers forming a pretend camera. She acted like she was taking a picture. "Snapshot!" she shouted. Then Renee looked at the make-believe camera as if she was checking the photo—guess it was an invisible digital—and teased, "Yikes, not your best face."

The dude's boys started laughing at him, and before he could say anything back, Renee said, "Next in line, please!"

Then he got all sensitive and cussed Renee up and down, throwing the typical "You ain't even that pretty anyway!" at her, bumping tables and chairs as he walked out. His boys trailed behind him like a litter of puppies. I looked down at my application as they were leaving. Guys like that always try to mess with somebody else to make them feel better, and I just wasn't in the mood.

Everyone else in line laughed, though. Especially when the next guy ordered fifty pieces of chicken and got every piece. Apparently, that's why she really couldn't sell that jerk the chicken. It was already spoken for.

"Thank you so much, love. I already have it squared with Clara," the man who ordered all the chicken said.

"No prob, Mr. Ray."

Mr. Ray? I looked up, and sure enough, it was Mr. Willie Ray standing there while Renee piled fried chicken into cardboard buckets.

Mr. Ray was a tall stick of a man who everyone in the neighborhood knew for two reasons. The first is, he was in the funeral business. A mortician. He owned Ray's Funeral Home after inheriting it from his father. It's weird to say, but most of the teenagers and old folks who've died around here have passed through Willie Ray's door.

The other thing everyone knows him for is, well, cancer. Mr. Ray beat it twice, and the only reason everybody knows that is because after he beat it the second time, he basically became, like, a Jehovah's Witness for cancer, knocking on doors and passing out pamphlets. He swears the only reason God spared his life twice is so that he could spread the word about the illness, as if nobody knew what it was. My mother used to always joke with him and say, "Willie, God saved you just so you could torture the hell outta the rest of us? That don't make no sense." He never got upset with her. He just used to laugh and shake his head while heading on to the next house.

"Mr. Ray?" I called out.

"Matthew, I didn't see you sitting there. How are you?" he said, walking toward me with his familiar limp.

"I'm okay." I stood and shook his hand. "What's with all the chicken?"

"Man, it's a funeral. Well, really it's a repast. They didn't have anyone to cater it, so they paid the funeral home extra for us to take care of the accommodations. So we always just come down here and get the chicken. It's easy and everybody likes it," he explained. "What you up to?"

"Just trying to get a job." I pointed to the application that I had literally only filled out my name on, so far.

"Where, here?"

"Yes sir."

Mr. Ray stood there for a second and gave me a once-over, as if he was upset that I was trying to work in Cluck Bucket. As far as I was concerned, it was an honest gig. I figured it was probably tough at times, but still, honest. Plus, I figured I could maybe learn what the secret to some of that fried deliciousness was so that I could take it back to my own kitchen. Maybe make those biscuits for me and my dad one day.

"Matthew, if you work here, you'll never be able to eat here again," he finally joked.

I didn't really think that was true. I mean, certain things you just never get tired of. Cluck Bucket, for me, was definitely one. That's like saying that if I would've gotten that job working at the bank, I would've eventually gotten sick of money. Yeah, right. Not that Mr. Ray was wrong. I just couldn't see it. But I didn't say nothing. Just shrugged.

"Listen. Your mother was a friend of mine. And your father still is. If you need a job, I'll pay you a couple of bucks to help me out down at the funeral home. I mean, I heard they pay pretty good in this crap shack, but I'm sure I can get close, and you won't have to come home smelling like deep-fried fat every night, or put up with these knuckleheads. What you think?" Mr. Ray inched his jacket sleeve up just enough to see his watch, which he twisted around so that the gold face was on the top of his wrist. "Unless," he said low, his eyes still on the time, "you got a thing for hairnets."